"Together?" Valerie and Cole said in unison.

Valerie cleared her throat. "But we're competing against each other."

"Whoever wins, the plaque will go on the Salty Dog storefront," Ava said.

"But the check...that will go in my account, right?" Valerie said.

"It's goin' in my account, darlin'." Cole turned to her with a slow smile.

"Don't bet on it, boss." But she added a little smile of her own.

"That's what I like to see," Ava said. "A little friendly competition."

Friendly? Cole was giving Valerie the side-eye. She well remembered that he was every bit as competitive as she was. More. This wouldn't be pretty.

* * *

CHARMING, TEXAS

Dear Reader,

Welcome to Charming, Texas, and the reunion between two people who have been unlucky in love. Cole and Valerie were each other's first loves, and fourteen years later, they will get their second chance at forever.

When Valerie discovers her grandmother is in financial trouble, she suggests that a woman should be allowed to enter the annual Mr. Charming contest, where residents compete for a sizable cash award. Valerie could use that money to help her grandmother. But Cole needs the money to make expensive repairs to his bar that are demanded by the Historical Society. These two competitive souls are far more alike than they are different, and it's all-out war to win the Mr. Charming contest. In the process, they will lose their hearts to each other. You saw that coming, right?

While I enjoyed researching the Gulf Coast and Galveston Bay, the town of Charming is completely fictional. This small town has a converted lighthouse, a boardwalk, a Ferris wheel, a bar and grill named the Salty Dog, and a dog named Submarine. You'll also meet the wonderful senior citizens who comprise the Almost Dead Poet Society and compose really bad poetry that might just make you smile.

Many thanks to my friend author Lisa Lewis Fenley, who read an early version of this book and gave comments and input on the area. I also want to thank all the wonderful readers who make it possible for me to do the best job in the world. I'm indebted to my private reader group, Heatherly's Belles. Reader Mary Smith named our hero's dog *Submarine* (*Sub* for short). And reader Phyllis Perryman named the seafood restaurant *The Waterfront*.

Thank you, Belles, I love you all! xoxo

Heatherly Bell

PS: I love to hear from you. You can reach me at heatherlybell@heatherlybell.com.

Winning
Mr. Charming

HEATHERLY BELL

HARLEQUIN
SPECIAL
EDITION

Recycling programs for this product may not exist in your area.

ISBN-13: 978-1-335-40492-3

Winning Mr. Charming

Copyright © 2021 by Heatherly Bell

This edition published by arrangement with Harlequin Books S.A.

For questions and comments about the quality of this book, please contact us at CustomerService@Harlequin.com.

Harlequin Enterprises ULC
22 Adelaide St. West, 40th Floor
Toronto, Ontario M5H 4E3, Canada
www.Harlequin.com

Printed in U.S.A.

Heatherly Bell tackled her first book in 2004, and now the characters that occupy her mind refuse to leave until she writes them a book. She loves all music but confines singing to the shower these days. Heatherly lives in Northern California with her family, including two beagles—one who can say hello and the other a princess who can feel a pea through several pillows.

Books by Heatherly Bell

Harlequin Special Edition

Wildfire Ridge

More than One Night
Reluctant Hometown Hero
The Right Moment

Harlequin Superromance

Heroes of Fortune Valley

Breaking Emily's Rules
Airman to the Rescue
This Baby Business

Visit the Author Profile page
at Harlequin.com for more titles.

For Jean Buscher

Chapter One

Cole Kinsella sat at a booth in the Salty Dog Bar & Grill, holding the application of one Valerie Hill. He needed a new server, but as he perused the résumé, he didn't see any recent experience listed. She'd last been employed as a third grade teacher in Missouri.

"She's a long way from home," Cole said to Sub, his yellow Lab, who lay sprawled on the floor.

With limited experience and all in the past, she was wasting her time, and he wondered why she wanted the job. The Salty Dog was busy on any given night as the only bar to serve both locals and tourists in Charming, Texas. Since he'd taken over, he'd kept most of the staff, but a couple of waitresses had recently quit. He didn't want to believe it, but if the rumors were true, they'd left because they believed the Salty Dog wouldn't be around much longer.

A few months ago, the Charming Historical Society had laid down the law. Make the required improvements to his establishment, or it would be shut down until such time as he complied. As the only bar in Charming, and a historical landmark, the Salty Dog was something that the society very much wanted to stay open. But those pesky repairs couldn't wait much longer.

He tapped his wristwatch. His prospective employee was two minutes late. Still, he reminded himself, two minutes wasn't a big deal to civilians. Just then the wooden double door opened, and a woman rushed inside, scanning the area. Beautiful and tall, with dark hair, she wore a short dress that revealed long legs that went on for a country mile. He rose to tell her they weren't open for another couple of hours, and his chest seized when he met her gaze. Her shimmering brown eyes were incredibly familiar.

Valerie. His Valerie.

He hadn't made the connection until now. Because he'd known Valerie Villanueva. Which meant she was married. Of course.

Did you really think she would still be single fourteen years later?

Predictably, Sub rose and began to whine, waiting for Cole to give him the hand command and permission to approach. But before Cole could, Valerie bent to pet Sub, making all the usual goo-goo phrases.

Hello, baby.

Aren't you precious?

Who's a good boy?

Then she stood to face him. "Hello, Cole."

Her soft lilt of a voice was also familiar, and he fought to keep from gaping. She might be a decade older, but she was still breathtaking.

"Hey, darlin'. That's Sub, short for Yellow Submarine, and he's usually in my back office. You here for the interview?" He beckoned her toward the table where her application waited.

The one listing limited waitressing experience.

"Yes."

"Been a long time." He waited until she sat first, then sat across from her, putting a safe distance between them.

"How've you been?" She met his eyes, and he caught no hint of anger in them.

There should be.

How to summarize fourteen years in a nutshell? He went for brevity. "Busy."

"So, uh…" She shifted in her seat. "You're probably wondering why I'm applying."

"Yup. No experience except in college? You're a teacher. Why would you want to work here?"

"I need the job. You remember my grandmother."

"Of course. Mrs. Villanueva." How could he forget? If not for Valerie's visits to see her grandmother in Charming every summer, they might have never met.

"She's been sick, as you've probably heard. I came

back to help take care of her. Cole, I *need* this job. And I waitressed in college at Mizzou, so it will all come back to me."

"You sure, sweetheart? It can get pretty crazy. We get a rowdy crowd in here sometimes. You do remember Texas?"

She slid him a look that told him she remembered. *Everything.*

"I can handle it. But I don't want you to give me this job because you feel like you owe me. Because you *don't.*"

He did. At the very least, an explanation. But he sure didn't owe her a job. "Okay. Then I don't—"

"Wait." She held up a palm. "I changed my mind."

"You don't want the job?"

"I think you should give me the job, or at least give me a *chance*, because we were…we were friends once." Her fingers drummed on the table. She seemed nervous, and she'd just rewritten history.

He fought a smile. By his definition, they were a bit more than friends. And he should not be thinking these randy thoughts about a married woman. But he got it. They'd both been eighteen that last summer. Kids. Stupid ones, at that. He was speaking for himself now.

Maybe he should give Valerie a chance. He remembered her as being enthusiastic and a quick learner. He'd taken her out on the water with him, and though she claimed she'd never been on a paddleboard before, she'd learned. Still, this said nothing about her waitressing skills. He would be taking a risk in hiring her. And for a new and struggling business owner, that might not be a great decision.

"How long are you going to be in Charming?" he asked, though this had nothing to do with the job. At the moment, he needed waitresses. In this business, he expected high turnover.

He was intrigued. Maybe she and Mr. Hill had a couple of children and he wondered how Valerie could stay away an entire summer.

"Just the summer. I'll go back to Columbia and my teaching job in the fall."

He thought about how many times he'd watched her leave at the end of the summer, figuring that nothing truly good in his life lasted. Two short months was all he ever got from her. Whether or not it made sense, he'd felt abandoned. Back then, he'd have given her a thousand jobs just to get her to stay. The least he could do was help her out for a short time, for old times' sake.

"Well, all right then, let's give this a try. Temporary trial basis to see how you work out. I'll get you an apron and you can start tonight." He stood, held out his hand and winked. "It's good to see you again, Mrs. Valerie Hill."

Her hand was small and warm in his and she squeezed back.

"Actually, I'm legally changing it back to Valerie Villanueva. I'm divorced."

* * *

Valerie hadn't meant to just blurt out the news. *How do you do? I'm Valerie, and I'm divorced. What's new with you?* Her Missouri driver's license, issued when she was married, had her ex-husband's last name. She'd never imagined there would be so much paperwork and time involved in an uncontested divorce.

"You're not going to be sorry about this. I promise."

He nodded and handed her an apron. "Good deal. See ya tonight."

She saluted. Not sure why. He blinked, so she quickly corrected and waved instead, then with one last pet to his beautiful dog she rushed outside into the hot and humid July afternoon before Cole could change his mind. That had gone well if she said so herself. She'd barely noticed that Cole had grown into his good looks. Now he wasn't a pretty surfer boy with his honey brown hair always golden at the tips. His dimples used to make him look boyish, now they were just plain sexy. He was tall and rugged, with sinewy forearms. She'd noticed a small scar under his left eyebrow. And he still owned an irresistible smile.

But she wasn't going to notice any of that.

She wasn't in Charming for him, or any man.

Valerie was here this summer for Patsy Villanueva, her father's mother, and the reason she'd enjoyed summers in Charming every year of her life growing up. When her parents had argued so con-tentiously before and *after* their divorce, Charming had been her escape. Her personal oasis.

The bucolic, small coastal town was everything she remembered. Picture-postcard perfect, with quaint lighthouses, bridges, jetties and piers jutting out to the sea along the wharf. Along the seawall-protected boardwalk were souvenir gift shops, a small amusement park with a roller coaster, and an old-fashioned Ferris wheel. Gram's favorite taffy shop, fine seafood dining and the Salty Dog.

The crisp aroma of the gulf filled the air, along with the tempting smells of her personal weakness. *Kettle corn*.

Valerie stopped by the saltwater taffy store for a bag of Gram's favorite peppermint-flavored candy and climbed in her Oldsmobile station wagon for the short drive to Woodland Estates, the seniors-only mobile home park. She'd been driving the beast be-cause it was the only vehicle available to her. Since she'd dropped everything after her grandmother's stroke, she'd left behind both her car and the apart-ment she'd moved into.

Valerie would have walked the scenic one-mile walk to the wharf or ridden her bicycle, but she hadn't wanted to be late to her interview with Cole. She'd managed to avoid him since she'd arrived six weeks ago, but when she heard he was hiring, there was no more avoiding Cole Kinsella.

She maneuvered the throwback Oldsmobile,

which had seen better years. As in the 1970s. It felt a bit like driving a boat. A yellow one with wood-panel stripping on the bottom and a sticker in the window that read I Ride with the Angels. God only knew how many miles were on this baby, because no doubt the speedometer had turned over a few times. It moved slowly, like an arthritic vehicle, if there were such a thing. Valerie wasn't even certain it could go above forty miles an hour.

She made her way toward her grandmother's home, dropping down to the five-mile-an-hour limit once she entered the park. The homes were tucked away in a lovely section of town, and from certain vista points one could see the nonoperational light-house. According to Gram, someone had converted it into a home and Cole currently lived there.

"Perfect timing," Lois Thornton, her grandmother's friend, said as she met Valerie at the front door. "I was just leaving. The therapist is inside, and Patsy already has her eyes closed. That faker. If you don't get in there soon, I'm sure she'll order another battery of tests Patsy doesn't really need."

Last week, her grandmother had pretended to be asleep and missed an entire physical therapy session.

"Thanks, Lois."

Inside, Gram sat in her favorite reclining chair, eyes closed, the therapist next to her with puckered lips and a tight frown on her face.

"I'm concerned," she said, catching Valerie's

gaze. "It's like we're regressing. She's suddenly so lethargic."

Yeah. Right.

"Hey, Gram. I'm home." Valerie placed a hand on her shoulder. "Guess what? I've got a job on the boardwalk. And I bought you some peppermint taffy."

Gram's dark eyes fluttered open, wide and dancing with amusement. "Sugar, that's so good to hear! A job!"

Valerie crossed her arms. "Lois said you were sleeping?"

Gram had the decency to look sheepish, rubbing her eyes. "Oh dear. I must have just drifted off there for a second." Then, as if just noticing the therapist, she said, "Oh, hello there."

"How are we today, Mrs. Villanueva?"

"I don't know about you. I'm fair to middlin'. Been better, but also been worse. Can't complain."

"Good, good. Now let's just see how those legs are doing today. We need to do our stretches, or we get weak, don't we? We can't have that. You want to be able to chase after those strong and handsome single men."

Gram grimaced, giving Valerie the stink eye.

"No pain, no gain." Valerie made her way into the kitchen where she started on the dishes from this morning's breakfast.

Listening to Gram curse in the background as she never had before she'd become acquainted with PT,

Valerie let her mind wander to her interview with Cole. She'd seen him in the distance a few times since she'd been in Charming, and once out on the water, where he practically lived. She had such sweet memories associated with him. Over the years, she'd thought of him now and then. Once, she'd looked him up online to check out his social media and find out if he'd ever been married.

As far as she could tell, he was still single. They'd been in love long ago, just kid stuff. She'd been foolish and was now a little embarrassed by that young, silly girl. It didn't make sense to still be attracted to him after all this time. Because that much had been obvious, given the way her heart had slammed against her rib cage the moment she'd shook his hand. *That* should not be happening. She hadn't planned for that at all. They'd both had very different opinions on their relationship status years ago, but she'd now been through a lot worse than the pain Cole Kinsella had put her through, and survived.

She'd get past this latest wrinkle, too.

Last week, while going through Gram's mail, she'd found a notice. She'd ripped open the envelope and been shocked to find that Gram owed several thousand dollars to Woodland Estates. She was behind on her space rental payments, plus the late fees that had accumulated. The Villanueva family had struggled for years, but they'd always gotten by with hard work. Her father had been the first to go to college, Valerie the second, and pride surrounded that accomplishment. Pride in knowing they didn't need to ask for assistance from anyone. Leave that for the far less fortunate, her grandfather used to say.

Valerie learned that her grandfather had always handled the bills. They were old school that way. In fact, the man had been so vigilant that he'd paid off the mortgage and some of the bills in advance for an entire year, knowing that he was ill, and might not survive the cancer diagnosis. Always taking care of his wife even in death. It would have been even better if he'd educated Gram instead.

Because he hadn't survived, and bills were the last thing on Gram's mind in her state of grief. Then the stroke had happened.

Gram had been sitting outside in her backyard enjoying sweet iced tea with her friends when she'd risen to get more cookies and fallen on the stone-paved patio. Her friends, all from the park, weren't strong enough to help her up. They'd dialed 911, to Gram's utter humiliation.

"Those good-looking young men came right on over, and I didn't know what to do sitting on the floor like I had good sense. There weren't enough cookies for them because I hadn't expected that much company. I just fanned and fanned mahself while I assured them I was just fine and dandy. But they wouldn't hear of it!"

"Good Lord, woman, do you come by being a sadist naturally or was this a skill you learned in school?" Gram now screeched. "My leg doesn't bend that way!"

Valerie winced with sympathy pain. The pushing and pulling of tight muscles must be agony, but it was the only way to get to the other side of mobility. Gram couldn't have her muscles atrophy and just give up on moving because it hurt too much. That would be the easy way out.

And the Villanuevas did not do easy.

Chapter Two

"This is going to cost you," said Ralph Mason, head contractor for the Historical Society. "I'm not going to sprinkle fairy dust on y'all, so gird your loins, now."

"Let me have it," Cole said, as he prepared to have his soul crushed.

Both he and Max Del Toro, his business partner and best friend, could wield a hammer and pound nails. But the Historical Society insisted that improvements be done by their chosen contractor to preserve the integrity of the building. It had taken most of Cole's savings and some of Max's simply to rescue the business from foreclosure. Cole was tapped out, and in real trouble if he couldn't figure out how to make those improvements the Charming Historical Society demanded.

Rumors that they'd be shut down had caused him to lose good help.

There were some good reasons to own a business in a historical district, since development was restricted. But special permits and licensed contractors were not some of those perks.

Ralph proceeded to list a litany of repairs, most of which came down to the roof that had not been properly fixed after a devastating category three hurricane decades ago. They'd already had rain this summer and Cole hadn't witnessed a single leak, but according to Ralph, they might soon be swimming in a sea of their own filth.

"Integrity is expensive," Cole grumbled, eyeing the estimate and trying not to clutch his heart.

"This is bullshit," Max said, far more eloquently.

"Tell me about it. If Lloyd had done even some of the improvements over the years, y'all might not be facing this situation. But one big storm and this roof might cave," Ralph said.

Life was one big party to Lloyd, Cole's father, so no wonder he'd put off doing the hard work.

Max wore his "I'm completely disgusted with you" scowl firmly in place. "How do I know you're not scamming us?"

"That's the beauty of this job, son," Ralph said. "The Historical Society knows I'm not scammin' ya, and that's all that matters."

"Great," Max muttered under his breath.

"How did Lloyd manage to put these off for so long?" Cole wanted to know.

Ralph gave him a patient look. "He must have *known* someone."

Yeah. And Cole would bet that "someone" was a woman.

After Ralph left, Cole and Max sat in the back office. Sub sat on his dog bed, chewing on a treat.

"Let me do a little more research," Max said. "I've got my eye on historical landmark grants. There are some available."

Cole stretched his legs out. "Probably a long line to get them, too."

"We obviously have zero equity to refinance at this point."

"Sorry I got you into this mess."

Lloyd was Cole's deadbeat father and he should have expected something like this to come out of trying to rescue the man

"Don't be," Max said. "You know that I don't get roped into stuff. The Salty Dog has the potential to be a cash cow. There's no further land development, so we'll never have any competition."

Even though Cole had set out to help Lloyd, big mistake, he hadn't done so without great advice. And if Max hadn't changed his mind about their investment, Cole wouldn't, either.

Later that afternoon, Cole observed Valerie as she flitted around from table to table. She'd arrived early for her shift, wearing jeans, a pink tank top and pink high-top sneakers. He'd handed her the new work uniform, a Salty Dog T-shirt with a photo of a salivating bulldog.

She'd simply smiled, said, "Really?" and pulled it over her top.

As the hours progressed, he was pleasantly surprised at how exceptional she was. He should have realized that her personal charm would translate to her work. From the other side of the room, where patrons were seated at tables for food, came raucous laughter.

"Oh, Mr. Collins, I will *never* get tired of that story." Valerie threw her head back in a hearty belly laugh. "I'll be back with y'all's drinks in just a jiffy."

"Take your time." Mr. Collins, one of their regulars, beamed. "No rush."

She crossed to the other side of the room and the bar. "Two domestics, three mai tais," she said to Cole.

"Comin' right up, darlin'." He grabbed two mugs from under the bar.

"How am I doin', boss?" She gave him a shoulder shimmy.

He did his job pretending that shimmy had absolutely zero effect on him. "Wish I had four more just like you."

"Aw, now, go on." She waved him away.

He set two drafts on her tray. "How's your grandma doin' these days, anyway?"

"Better as long as she doesn't keep fighting the physical therapy. Tonight, one of her friends from the trailer park is looking in on her. I hate to leave her alone for long."

"She's that bad off?"

She shrugged. "I'm overprotective."

Finished mixing the drinks, he set them on her tray, then watched with no small amount of trepidation as she balanced and carried them back to the table. He shouldn't have worried. The Valerie he remembered worked hard to excel at everything. There were summer days when she'd bring along her advanced course reading to the beach. She had perfect grades and attendance. She was a good granddaughter and friend. As he recalled, an amazing kisser.

Definitely too good for him. He'd been way out of his league from day one and realized it. But he just couldn't back down. Not until he'd been forced to do it. If she was holding that against him, there seemed to be no evidence so far. But why would she? She'd obviously gotten over him, fallen in love and married someone.

Cole was polishing a glass when a funny thing happened. Valerie delivered the cocktails with a huge smile, patting Mr. Collins on the shoulder. As soon as she left, some of the customers switched drinks with each other. They didn't seem at all put out by the mistake.

Not so perfect after all, are you, baby?

Yeah, he would keep her. One more summer. Then

she'd be gone again. He ought to warn his customers not to get too attached. Valerie already had half the crowd in love with her. She smiled and chatted and hustled for those tips.

His old classmate Penny Richards came in alone again, wearing, as usual, as little as possible. Seemed to be some kind of a dress with half of it missing. Damn, he loved south Texas summers.

"Hey, Penny. What's doin'?"

"Hey, there. I'll have a mojito." She set her purse down on the empty stool next to her.

It wouldn't be empty long if he knew Penny. "Mojito comin' right up."

"Got somethin' for ya." Penny slid a paper across the bar.

As he crushed mint leaves, he glanced at the flyer. "What's that?"

Penny batted her eyelashes. "Why, it's the Mr. Charming contest. I think you could win, hands down. You're definitely charming. *And* sexy."

"Aw, thanks, sweetheart." He and Penny flirted, but both knew he'd never be one in her long line of conquests.

"This is the contest your father won every year, until…well, *you* know."

"Yeah." The less said about that, the better.

Suffice it to say, his father hadn't been a great businessman. He'd gambled away most of his profits.

"It comes with a ten-thousand-dollar purse."

Cole had been crushing ice in the blender, so he wasn't sure he'd heard right. "*How* much?"

"How do you think Harry renovated his shop last year? And, sweetheart, I need this place to stay open. It's the only bar in Charming."

Hell, *he* needed this place to stay open. He hadn't sunk his savings into it to have it close down because of some hoity-toity Historical Society rule. But *Mr. Charming*? He thought the contest was phony and ridiculous, *especially* because his father had won, but that was before he heard three little words.

Ten thousand dollars.

At the end of her shift, Valerie's feet felt like two blocks of cement. First, they felt as though someone had struck a match and lit them on fire. Later in her shift, like someone had taken a hammer and nail to her soles. And she'd thought teaching third grade was difficult. It was tough to smile when her feet were killing her, but smile she did. And chat. Flirt. It was easy in a way because the residents of Charming came by their town's name honestly.

They were kind and welcoming and didn't skimp on gratuities. Now she consoled herself by counting those tips, then putting them away carefully in the top dresser drawer in her bedroom. A few more nights like these and she'd put a dent in those space rental payments and late fees. She had to have a serious talk with Gram tonight about the bills, about asking for help, but that would have to wait until after poetry group.

Gram watched TV while Valerie tidied up the living room. Straightened books. Fanned out magazines. Put away clutter. She set out the cookies and the pitchers of punch and iced tea on the coffee table. Tonight was the weekly gathering of the Almost Dead Poets Society reading group. Ever since Gram's stroke, they'd all decided to meet at her home to facilitate logistics.

The first time Valerie heard the founder, Etta May Virgil, recite her poem *Ode to Buttermilk*, she'd understood that no one here considered themselves a great laureate. Like with so many other of their recreations—bingo, karaoke night and sit-ercise—the seniors had fun and kept busy. Unfortunately, Gram's poems about her late husband verged on erotic—a torture for Valerie. At least they were nearly erotic from Valerie's perspective, but she was a prude. And this was her *grandmother*. She didn't like to believe that her grandmother had ever even *had* sex, much less that she missed having it with her husband. Ew.

Valerie slunk further in her seat as Gram read tonight's poem about deep wet kisses and warm hugs in the rain. It was awful, and Valerie meant that in the most loving way. But she'd bet that had it been up to Gram, the group *should* have been called the Fifty Shades of Gray-Haired Grannies.

"Bravo, Patsy!" Etta May clapped. "Bravo! Thank

you for another poem that reminds us how we must love deeply, while we still can."

"We are the *almost* dead poets." Lois snorted and elbowed Valerie.

"Don't say that," Valerie hissed. "You're only as old as you feel."

"Sugar, my doctor said my new hip will last me ten *years*. When he said that, I realized that my hip might actually outlive the rest of me. Maybe my daughter can sell it for the spare parts." She giggled. "Oh, Lord, that's too morbid, even for me."

Valerie closed her eyes and pinched the bridge of her nose. She was substantially uplifted and taken away from thoughts of titanium hips, spare parts and the inevitability of death when Susannah Ferguson began to read her poem about her cockapoo, Doodle.

Doodle, Doodle.

You're my little poodle.

I love you oodles and oodles.

That's why your name is Doodle.

The poem went on, all rhyming, with Susannah extolling the virtues of her doggy. To be fair, this was difficult to do while rhyming every line. Valerie restrained the laughter that threatened to bubble up. She bit her lower lip because everyone else was so moved by Susannah's tribute.

"That's wonderful." Gram patted Susannah's knee. "I think about getting a dog all the time."

"Maybe after Valerie goes home. You'll need the company," Susannah said.

This caused a general ruckus, senior-citizen style.
Valerie's leaving?
Who said?
What? When? Why?

Lois passed around a tray of her tea sandwiches. "Don't be silly. Valerie wouldn't *leave*. This is Texas. Nobody leaves unless they're forced to."

"I'll have to leave at the end of summer when school starts again."

She'd committed herself to teaching years ago and had a solid career she loved. Her school, community and students all depended on her. Valerie had accepted a new contract in April before Gram's stroke, and she'd have to honor that.

"We need to match you up with a hot-blooded Texan man!" Susannah clapped. "Maybe a cowboy."

Valerie didn't need a man. No, thanks. She was fiercely independent and never tried anything bold or rash anymore. Her life was calm and routine and that was the way she liked it. The last time she'd tried to do anything crazy, exciting… Well, she didn't want to think about that right now.

"That's going to be a little tough since she's not dating," Gram said pointedly.

"Poor darlin' got burned something fierce by her ex-husband," Lois said, offering more sandwiches to Valerie.

What the heck. Valerie loaded up on cucumber and cream cheese. "I don't want to talk about it."

"What she needs is a Gulf Coast man. One with

a Southern drawl and the corresponding upstanding morals from the land of the men without peers." This came from Roy Finch, the only man in the group. He'd agreed to join the ladies only if they'd change the name of the poetry group from Red Hot Seniors.

Mr. Finch's poems never rhymed, and they were always about the evils of corporate oil machines and the damage they'd done to the fields of his beloved Texas. His poems were often the most interesting of the group, because he enacted the voices of inanimate objects and…Texas. Valerie didn't think they would win any literary prize, but they kept *her* interest. She wondered what he'd make other states sound like. Texas sounded like a pissed-off giant on an emphysema oxygen tank.

Finally, after the poetry readings were over and everyone had retired to their own homes, Valerie sat watching TV with Gram.

"What did you think of Mr. Finch offering to fix you up with a Gulf Coast man?" Gram asked during a commercial for dog food.

Maybe I should get a dog. Cole and Sub seemed to be so simpatico with each other.

"He did not offer to fix me up, Gram."

"But, sugar, if you don't get back on the horse again, you might forget how to ride."

"Ugh." Valerie covered her face with her hands. "Just what I want to hear from my own grandmother."

"I don't want you to wind up *bitter*, *mija*."

"At least you didn't say 'a bitter divorcée.' Look, maybe I've done enough riding for a while."

"There are plenty of good men out there. Just because you got a dud doesn't mean you give up on love. The best revenge is to be happy again. To live."

"I *am* living. A person doesn't have to be in a relationship to have a life."

All she'd ever wanted was a committed and loving relationship with a wonderful man. A loyal man. Her grandparents had been the only example she'd seen of lasting love. And she'd wanted that for herself. She'd wound up with Greg instead.

Finally, the commercials ended and they went back to their show.

Valerie wondered how much longer she'd have to deal with people thinking they knew better than she did what she needed. Greg had always fought to control her, and, finally realizing he couldn't, found someone else. Regina, who was about as independent as a newborn puppy. Even now, he was still trying to control Valerie with the house they'd owned together. Two years later, she was living in an apartment with a roommate and Greg still hadn't sold the house. It had been in the divorce settlement to sell, but then he'd offered to buy her out. Valerie accepted. Later, claiming problems qualifying for a loan, he went back and forth, refusing to sell until she'd threatened him with going back to court.

That had been the persuasion needed for him to agree to put the house up for sale earlier this month.

If he'd only done so sooner, she could have used some of her funds to help Gram out of this mess. Now, it was tied up in escrow for at least thirty days.

She would go back to Missouri after she helped get Gram out of this financial hole and resume her life. Maybe buy something smaller for herself. A condo instead of another house.

Once school started at the end of summer, her life would resume its schedule. She'd adopt a dog, probably a little one that wouldn't be too much trouble. At school, she'd continue to hang out with her colleagues. There would be many school events, conferences, get-togethers and parties she'd attend where it wouldn't matter that she was alone.

"I think I'll get myself to bed," Gram said, standing and grabbing on to her walker.

"We need to talk." Valerie stood, ready to assist if needed.

"You keep sayin' that."

"And you keep avoiding this talk."

"Because I know what you're going to say, and the answer is no. Absolutely not."

"There's nothing *wrong* with asking for help. You were grieving and didn't know what you were doing. Then you had the stroke. It's no wonder you're in financial trouble."

"*Chica*, your grandfather never asked for anyone's help. Not a day in his life. He worked hard, and that's the Villanueva way. We don't take charity."

"It's not charity to ask your only son for help!"

"No. I refuse. He knows how his father and I felt about divorce. And what does he do? Gets himself another wife when he already had one. You and your poor mami. For shame!" She then uttered a slew of Spanish curse words which she only did when superbly angry.

Valerie didn't bother to explain that her mother had recovered long ago. Even if she'd never worked outside of the home until the divorce, she'd studied to become a nurse and loved her job.

"I'm not exactly thrilled with him, either, you know. But he's your son and no matter what, Gram, I know he loves you. He was devastated when Papa died."

Her tiny grandmother, five foot nothing, reached up with one hand and touched Valerie's face. "*Mi amor*, we will figure this out without Rob. You'll see."

Despite the fact that Valerie didn't think there were enough tips in the entire state of Texas for her to dig Gram out of this hole in time, she listened. To her grandmother, this was about respect, right or wrong. Valerie understood.

Like it or not, she would have to accept this.

Her father would not be asked to help. No one would be asked.

And she was reminded, once again, that the Villanuevas did not do easy.

Chapter Three

The sun broke over the horizon just as Cole locked the front door of the converted lighthouse he lived in, Sub right behind him. A few minutes later he arrived at his favorite spot on the beach and pulled his board off the back of his truck's bed. He and Sub loved to start the morning with a run at the waves. Sub's favorite things in the world were: bacon, water and belly rubs. In that order.

There were already other diehards at the one area where a surfer could get a decent swell on the Gulf Coast in the summertime. The best time for waves in the gulf was right before a hurricane, but only those with balls of steel attempted that. Cole had tried it…once.

Max Del Toro stalked out of the water, holding his board. He nodded in Cole's direction.

They usually met here two or three times a week. Two former navy SEALs, close as brothers, and neither one of them could stay out of the water for long. Fortunately, Max didn't do small talk.

Cole nodded at the regulars and wasted no time joining Max for another run at the waves. Sub was already in the breaks, chasing waves like a sheep dog. The sky was a swirl of deep and fiery red, which meant rain could be on its way. No surprise there. The rain at least brought about a temporary reprieve from the heat. He spent the hour enjoying the morning, grateful that the water wasn't sauna-hot yet. The gulf was definitely an acquired taste.

Tourists said being in the water felt a bit like swimming in a huge hot tub. Some didn't care for it at all and headed for a swimming pool to cool off. He understood. But Cole had been all over the world with the US Navy and his SEAL team, in every sea and ocean. He'd been in near-arctic-weather swimming conditions and in tropical ones. And he'd choose the Gulf Coast every single time. This was home.

An hour later, he toweled off and changed out of his board shorts within the confines of the towel he held up the way only a surfer could manage without dropping. A few feet away, Max did the same.

"Any word?" Cole asked.

"Nope."

He didn't know why he bothered asking. Max would let him know when and if they obtained a grant for the improvements. Until then, they'd have to keep asking for more time and hope they got it.

Charming's boardwalk was waking up when he arrived, parked and made his way to the bar. The Salty Dog was at the end of the boardwalk and past the Ferris wheel and storefronts opening up for another day of tourism. An ice cream shop that served the best waffle cones on the coast was kitty-corner to the Ferris wheel. A souvenir gift store next to them sold magnets in the shape of Texas and a good selection of cowboy hats. The Lazy Mazy Kettle Corn on the corner was a store popular with locals.

As usual, Sub occasionally barked a greeting to his favorite people.

"Hey, there, Cole," said Harry from the saltwater taffy store as he rolled up his cage. "Don't ya worry, I'm not entering Mr. Charming this year. It's quite enough for me to be the winner three years runnin'. Least that's what the wife says."

"Givin' someone else a chance, are ya?"

"Yessir, and I heard that might be you."

"Throwin' my hat in the ring." He shrugged. "What the hell."

Last night, he'd decided to get over his damned self.

He wasn't anything like Lloyd Kinsella, and anyone with half a brain could see that. Cole hadn't even met the man until he was eighteen and about to ship off with the navy. And what a shock to learn dear old dad had been living in Houston, not far from Charming, where Cole had grown up with his mother, Angela.

His relationship with the old man had been tenuous at best. But then Cole's mother had passed away and Lloyd became the only real family Cole had left. He'd accepted Lloyd's apology for abandoning him when he'd promised to make up for the lost time.

So far, Lloyd hadn't done too well in that department. Instead Cole continually did all the heavy lifting, often literally. Lloyd didn't understand that Cole wanted a relationship with his father that didn't just involve driving the man home when he was too stinkin' drunk to do it himself. He needed a father, not a buddy. He'd had plenty of buddies, some that had laid down their lives for him. No one could compete with that.

Reminding himself that Lloyd's shortcomings didn't matter anymore because Cole only needed his tribe, which he already had, he kept walking down the plank wood floor.

"Hey, there, how are you doin', darlin'?" he called out to Karen, who managed The Waterfront, the fine dining seafood restaurant two storefronts down from the bar and grill.

Sub barked, as she was one of his favorite people.

"I'm good, honey. Thanks for the advice. I told Eric he either puts a ring on it, or I'm goin' off to greener pastures, if you catch my drift."

"Aw, you're too good for him." He pointed and winked. "You be sure to call me if it doesn't work out with good ol' Eric."

She smiled and waved him away. "Oh, go on, now."

Karen was a good fifteen years older than him. She knew Cole didn't mean anything by it. He was just a flirt by nature. Why not? Flirting was fun and as long as he wasn't hurting anyone, he didn't see the harm in it. One of the best parts about bartending, besides the flirting, was all the listening he got to do. He was surprisingly good at it. People told him their troubles and he did his best to offer solutions. Sometimes, only the listening was required.

A few hours later, Cole had settled Sub in the back office with his food, water and chew toys, and received a shipment of imported beer from his distributor and the fish order for his head cook, Nick—who should have been there to receive it.

Nick rolled in just before noon, his apron slung over his shoulder. "What a night! And morning."

"The redhead?" Cole had seen him leaving with a tall, long-legged woman the previous evening.

He imitated an arrow piercing his heart. "I don't know, man, this might be it for me. The one."

"Yeah, right."

Nick claimed that was the case once a week, but he was a total player and fooling no one. Cole had been there, done that, and grown the hell up. After one disastrous engagement, he knew better than to mess around with a woman unless he had every intention of following through. This meant he hadn't dated anyone since he arrived back to Charming, but he also hadn't met anyone that stirred his interest even slightly.

The place woke up as workers began to arrive, waving hello and clocking in. He found himself waiting for Valerie to walk inside. She was on the schedule for the earlier shift today. He wondered what had happened between her and Mr. Hill the idiot. Although he shouldn't be so judgy. Cole and Mr. Hill had something in common. They'd both lost Valerie.

Cole walked to the door to turn the sign from Closed to Open, and got nearly hit in the face with the door as it swung open violently, and Valerie ran smack into the middle of his chest. Instinct had him reaching to stop her forward momentum, and he wound up with his hands around her upper arms. Damn, she smelled good. A hard and unwelcome pull of lust punched through his body.

"Oh, Lord. I'm sorry!" She rubbed her forehead.

"I'm fine. Are *you*? You hit my chest pretty hard with your…head."

"Um, yeah. I am." She met his gaze, her brown eyes shimmering.

Awkwardly, he slid both hands down her arms and removed them.

"I guess I better go clock in." She swung past him.

He got busy behind the bar as tourists and regulars gradually began to file in for the lunch hour. They were also short a hostess, so Cole filled in and did the work. Sometimes from behind the bar.

"Anywhere is fine," he said to a family of four that looked ready for a day at the beach.

They sat at Valerie's table and to her credit, she was there to greet them less than a minute later. "Hi, folks. Where y'all from?"

He watched her now as she buzzed around the room, taking orders and chatting it up.

But he couldn't shake the feeling that Valerie could put on a hell of a show. She seemed to have everything together but obviously something had gone wrong in her life plans. She was divorced and taking care of her sick grandmother. Working as a waitress for the summer when she was a schoolteacher. What had gone wrong in the intervening years?

He shouldn't be this curious.

I never want to see you again, Cole.

Those words were bullets that had pierced his lovesick heart at the time.

He'd just put up another round of drafts for table four when Ava Long, president of the Chamber of Commerce, waltzed into the room and right up to the bar.

"Hey, Ava. How's things?"

"Tell me it's true. Please do tell."

"Love to. What are we talkin' about?" He gave the counter a wipe.

"You're entering Mr. Charming." She set a single form in front of him and folded her hands.

"Word travels fast. Was just thinkin' of dropping by later to see what's up. Where do I sign?"

She touched the paper. "Right there."

He glanced at the form. Name. Establishment. Place of birth. Birth date. "That simple, huh?"

"That simple and that complicated. You *will* have some stiff competition this year. Tanner over at the Lazy Mazy may just give you a run for your money. He turned twenty-one, so he just made the cutoff."

"Yeah," Cole scoffed. "Tanner."

That kid thought he was God's gift to women. The way he carried himself, you wouldn't know that he worked at the Lazy Mazy Kettle Corn. He was a charmer, all right. Might be Cole's biggest competition. If he hadn't already decided on entering, this news would have clinched it.

Cole signed his name and pushed the paper back. "Bring it *on*."

"Wonderful. I'm so excited! This will be our best year yet. Mr. Charming is in its sixtieth year, but this is the first year I'm spearheading the event." She thumped her chest proudly.

This might be as good a time as any to ask. "So… um, what do I have to do, exactly?"

"Just be charming twenty-four seven. I'll be putting up a sign in your window that says you're participating. This is all about drumming up tourism, and whoever wins will be the face of Charming for the next year. Residents vote online, and in a month, the new Mr. Charming is elected. It's a lot of fun, and each establishment will hold one townwide event in which they announce they're participating."

This suddenly wasn't sounding easy and that event wasn't in the fine print. "An *event*?"

"Actually, this is the first year we're doing the event, because I'm determined to spruce this contest up just a tad." She raised her arms in the air like a champ. "Put my own stamp on it. It's going to be *fun*!"

"Yeah," Cole said, pasting on a smile. "Fun."

Ava turned to the waning after-lunch crowd. "Everyone, may I have your attention? Cole Kinsella has just signed up to be an entrant for our annual Mr. Charming contest. Let's give him our support and may the best mister win."

There was a short round of applause and smiles from the customers. But Valerie had simply stopped, holding a tray she'd just emptied of its entrées.

Hand on her hip, she asked, "What's Mr. Charming?"

Chapter Four

Things got weirdly quiet when Valerie asked about this Mr. Charming business. Cole turned his back to her and got busy behind the bar. The petite blonde woman who'd come in and made the announcement with the energy of a Dallas Cowboys cheerleader waltzed up to Valerie.

"Hi, sweetie, are you new here?"

"Hey, there. I'm Valerie Villanueva from Missouri."

"You must be Patsy's granddaughter. Welcome to Charming!"

She shook Valerie's hand and spoke with the enthusiasm Valerie usually reserved for holidays, weddings and Christmas Day.

"I'm Ava Long. Mr. Charming is a Charming, Texas, *tradition*. Every year, the merchants and workers of Charming compete for the title. The winner gets an engraved plaque put in the window of their establishment and ten thousand dollars to help grow or improve their place of business. Or perhaps an owner might want to reward their staff with a huge party. Whatever they like. It's just about being kind, friendly, welcoming. *Charming.*"

Valerie blinked. "I'm sorry, did you say ten *thousand* dollars?"

"Yes, I did."

"Can the person who wins use the money for anything they'd like?"

"Of course. Last year the winner took his family on a fancy cruise. The money is for the winner to do as he wishes, but most use it for business improvements. That's mostly the point. It's just that he won three years in a row and pretty much had already improved everything he could on his shop."

"Who can enter this contest?"

She laughed and waved her hand. "Well, it's *Mr.* Charming, so…"

"Wait. There's no Ms. Charming contest? Or Miss Charming?"

"Well, no…" She riffled through the briefcase she had with her that seemed to be filled with flyers. "It's always been Mr. Charming."

"Wow. That seems kind of…shortsighted?"

"Huh?" Ava simply stared. "How do you mean?"

"Let me guess." Valerie crossed her arms. "This contest has been going on for several decades. And in all that time, a woman has never wanted to enter."

"I never… I never… It's just…" Ava sputtered.

"Now that I think about it, that doesn't seem quite fair." Debbie, another waitress, came up behind Valerie. "I wouldn't want to enter because it's insulting to think I should have to be *charming* to win a thing. But why can't a woman enter if she wants?"

"It's *Mr.* Charming," Ava said.

"Maybe it shouldn't be." Valerie considered how that money would go a long way toward paying off some of Gram's many bills.

"But everything is already printed up and ready to go. All the plaques say *Mr.*" Ava didn't sound like Christmas Day anymore. "It's always been done this way."

"Somethin' to be said for tradition," a male customer said. "Why not stay in your own lane?"

The woman he was with shot him a glare.

Someone from Valerie's table, Mrs. Jones, stood, hands on hips. "I suggest you let a *woman* enter the Mr. Charming contest."

"I would love to enter," Valerie said, hand to heart. "And I'll win."

Ava looked as though a pack of wolves had descended on her. "I'll have to talk to someone. Maybe the mayor. I don't know. I—"

"Ava, you're the president, and didn't you say this was your first year spearheading the event?" This was from Cole, who hadn't said a word until then. He'd come around from behind the bar to stand beside Ava.

"Y-yes."

"*You're* in charge, sweetheart." He slid his big arm around Ava's shoulders. "This could be your defining moment. No need for an *event*. Just think of how progressive an idea this is. Our mayor's going to love it And it will have your stamp of individuality all over it. Of *course* a woman can be *Mr.* Charming. Of course."

Ava glanced up at him adoringly. Valerie frowned, certain that look had nothing to do with his little speech and everything to do with him touching her. Ava had it bad for Cole Kinsella. Who didn't?

Boy, could that man sweet-talk. She sure remembered all the tender words he'd once whispered to her. Valerie would never want him anywhere but on her side. Wait. If she entered Mr. Charming, she'd be competing with…Cole. *The* single most charming man she'd probably ever met.

Trying to take away *her* $10,000.

"It's not like there are stringent bylaws for this contest or a manual of practices and procedures." Ava chewed on her lower lip. "It's just meant to help businesses like when we vote every year for our favorite bank, restaurant, that kind of thing."

"Exactly," Cole said, not removing his arm. "No harm done."

"Well, sure, I *guess* it would be all right. Even if it's a little…weird."

"It's not a *little* weird." This was from the same ornery man.

Everyone ignored him. All the women, and some of the men, clapped. Ava dug in her briefcase and handed Valerie a form. "Fill this out, pay your entry fee, and you're in."

"Thanks so much!" Valerie turned to her table section, waving the form. "This is so exciting. I appreciate your support and hope that you'll vote for me. You want charming? You got it! I'm going to be the best waitress y'all have ever had."

Cole then turned to Ava, who still stood next to him, reveling in the closeness while it lasted, Valerie assumed.

"There's no need for us to have an event, then? Yeah? You've already put your mark on the contest. No one's ever going to forget this," Cole said.

"Well, I don't know about *that*. Events are such fun. And just think. Now you and your lovely waitress can coordinate together." Ava waved her hand between them.

Cole's arm slid off Ava and his eyes narrowed.

"Together?" Valerie and Cole said in unison.

Valerie cleared her throat. "But we're competing against each other."

"Whoever wins, the plaque will go on the Salty Dog storefront," Ava said.

"But the check…that will go in my account, right?" Valerie said.

"It's goin' in my account, darlin'." Cole turned to her with a slow smile.

"Don't bet on it, boss." But she added a little smile of her own.

"That's what I like to see," Ava said. "A little friendly competition."

Friendly? Cole was giving Valerie the side-eye. She well remembered that he was every bit as competitive as she was. More. This wouldn't be pretty.

Once Ava was gone, Valerie got back to waiting on her tables. She'd always hustled for her tips, but this time she added in news of her running in the Mr. Charming contest. Feedback was mixed. The older crowd, her favorites, were a little confused but got right on board once she explained. She'd talk to Gram and get the Almost Dead Poets Society to endorse her. They were some of her most fervent supporters.

Later, she waited at the bar until Cole set her drink orders down. She'd been on her feet for eight hours. Her feet ached, and she longed to go home and take a nice long soak in the bath.

"Need to talk to you."

Oh, Lord, *no*. Was he going to fire her so she couldn't compete against him? If so, that was a nasty, terrible thing to do and she'd shout it from the rooftops. Then she'd just get a job anywhere else, even as a shampoo girl at the hair salon, and proceed to mop the floor with Cole Kinsella.

"About what? Mixing up the drink orders? No one seems to mind but I promise to do better." She gave him her most flirty, customers-only smile.

"Yeah, not that. Meet me in my office after you clock out."

He was going to fire her! "Oh. Okay."

Valerie was so scared she'd lose her job that she gave Debbie a hug and slid her a slip of paper with her cell phone number on it. It was hard to find good girlfriends—oh, how she knew that—and Valerie felt good about Debbie, who was sweet and supportive. They closed up for the night and Valerie was the last to leave. Cole had headed into his office thirty minutes ago and she'd stalled for as long as she could.

Now or never. She rapped lightly on the door and walked into a wood-paneled office. A surfboard stood in the corner of the room. Otherwise, there was just a desk, a couple of chairs and a short leather love seat in front of a coffee table. In one corner, Sub lay on what appeared to be a comfortable dog bed. He panted, and Valerie would swear he smiled, but he didn't get up.

"He's trained not to get up unless I give him a signal," Cole explained.

"Hi, Sub," she said to him anyway, never one to ignore a dog. She then turned to Cole. "Y-you wanted to see me?"

"Yeah." Cole sat behind the mahogany desk. "Sit down, please."

She did, because her feet hurt, and for no other reason. Not that she would tell him that. Let him think she had feet made out of lead. "Cole, please don't fire me. I—"

He held up a palm in the universal gesture for "stop." "You think I'm going to *fire* you? What kind of a creep do you think I am?"

"Um…oh, I don't think you're a creep. Not at all. But…maybe you really want to win."

An easy smile slid across his handsome face, dimples flashing through the light beard scruff. "You think the only way I can win is by firing you."

She hesitated, then went for naked honesty. "Yes?"

He chuckled. "I'll win and I'll win honestly. You're welcome, by the way. I talked Ava into letting you enter. Why would I do that if I was afraid of the competition?"

"Yeah, hate to burst your bubble, but Ava agreed because she has a thing for you. It wasn't your great argumentative skills."

He leaned back in his chair and crossed his arms. "Ava does not have a *thing* for me."

Okay, so he was *charmingly* oblivious. She snorted. "Yeah. Okay, then."

When he didn't speak but simply continued to stare, she squirmed. "So you're not firing me?"

"No. But we should talk about how we'll want to

keep the peace around here. It wouldn't do to have our regulars watch us slug it out day after day."

"I agree. We need to be nice to each other. Charming, even. That's the point."

"There's something else you should consider. Ava was fairly easy to convince, and so were our regulars, but it may be different for the rest of the town. We're rather stuck in our ways around here at times. Small town."

"If you're trying to psych me out, please don't. I've been through far worse."

He quirked a brow. "What I'm trying to say is that given you're not a *mister*, it might be hard for some of the residents to actually vote for you."

"I'll just work harder to make my case." She leaned forward. "And I should warn you. I've probably got the support of the Almost Dead Poets Society already in the bag."

He blinked. "The *what*?"

"Just a group of senior citizens who love me about as much as all women love you."

He scowled. "That's a good point. We'll split the vote down the middle, men voting for you, women for me."

"Except for the senior citizens. I think even the women will vote for me, thank you very much."

"Listen, I have a suggestion. Maybe we could agree to split the prize money, whoever wins."

He was quaking in his boots. Hunky Cole Kinsella was on the ropes. She had him. "That's okay. I want to do this on my own."

"Right." He met her gaze and oh, Lord, she'd forgotten his *eyes*. They were penetrating. A deep ocean-blue. "But want to tell me why you need this money? Maybe I can help."

Oh, hell to the no, he felt *sorry* for her. He wasn't worried she might win. He was worried she *wouldn't* and so had offered to split the prize. Of all the nerve.

She laughed bitterly. "Don't worry, I'm not on the run from the cartel or anything like that."

"Funny." He stood, all six feet or so of hard body oozing testosterone all over the place. "If you're in trouble of any kind, the ex-husband looking for you, anything, I *want* to know."

"So what, you can kill him?" She crossed her arms and studied the floor. "My ex-husband isn't looking for me, I can assure you."

"What am I supposed to think, Vallie? You show up here, years later, divorced, a schoolteacher who wants to work as a waitress, and I'm not supposed to ask any questions?"

No one had ever called her *Vallie* before or since. Her heart squeezed tight with the memory.

"Why do I need to be in *trouble* to want the money? Maybe I'd just like to have a little plastic surgery or something and feel like a new woman after my divorce."

He narrowed his eyes. "You better not."

"I'll do what I want, *Cole*."

He sighed deeply. "You always have. Bottom line?

You're beautiful and the customers already adore you. Safe to say that you'll probably beat me."

She stood. When he moved closer, she had to resist the urge to back up. But big and brawny though he was, Cole didn't intimidate her. He emitted rays of smoldering heat that were hotter than a Texas summer. They were piercing her in tender places that she hadn't explored in a while. In that moment she realized what a formidable opponent she had before her.

His smile was wicked. "Just don't expect me to make it easy for you, sweetheart."

"I'd expect nothing less than everything you've got, baby." Two could play at this game.

His head snapped back ever so slightly at the endearment.

He was right. At some point, they would need to talk about their past. About how they'd left things between them. Bitter. Since she'd arrived, the tension between them had simmered on low flame as they both ignored their shared past. He was the boss and she was the waitress and she'd believed the rest could be ignored.

Now they were in each other's sights with steadfast, laser focus. They each wanted the same bright and shiny prize. He was going to turn on the charm full blast and she was going to do the same. She couldn't back down. It wasn't in her DNA. She was a Villanueva through and through.

But Cole Kinsella would not back down, either.

Chapter Five

Two mornings later, Valerie stood at the stove frying up some bacon and eggs for Gram when she prepared to announce her latest news. With the next poetry meeting coming up in a few days, Valerie wanted Gram to be prepared when she asked for everyone's support.

"So…did I tell you that I'm entering the Mr. Charming contest?"

She chuckled. "That's funny, *mija*. That contest is for men."

"Did you ever ask yourself why?" Valerie flipped an egg.

"Not really. It's just always been that way. What does it matter, anyway? It's just another way to help local business owners."

"But the winner gets ten thousand dollars and they don't necessarily have to use it for their business. Anyone can win."

"Is it *that* much?"

"I'm going to win that contest, and I'm going to use the money to pay your past due space rent and all the late fees. Maybe fix some things up around here, too."

"Oh, no, sugar. I can't let you to do that. If you win, *you* take the money. You'll need it to start over."

If she won? Gram hadn't been acquainted with Valerie's resolve in a while. One would think that her dropping everything to come care for Gram would have given her a hint. She didn't roll over and play dead.

"You forget I've got half of the house in Missouri that Greg and I owned. And as soon as it sells, I'll have that chunk to start over."

Honestly, the minimal amount that Gram knew about finances was kind of frightening. Valerie was going to educate her bit by bit.

"Well, use it to do...*something* for yourself. You need to remember that you're a young lady that shouldn't spend all of her free time with us old folks."

"But I love you old folks." Valerie slid a plate of bacon, sunny-side-up eggs and hash browns in front of Gram.

Gram harrumphed and picked up her fork. "That's because we're safe. None of us are going to break your heart."

"Let's not talk about my broken heart when there are so many more serious problems around here for us to deal with." Valerie sat, cradling her morning cup of coffee.

"Keep a positive attitude. Everything will work itself out in time." Gram patted Valerie's hand. "Your grandfather used to say so, and somehow it always did."

Probably because he'd worked out a plan and didn't want to bother his wife's pretty little head about it. Valerie would never wind up like Gram. So dependent on a man for…everything. Did Gram really think positive thoughts made money appear?

"Anyway, I'm going to ask the poetry club to support me."

"Sure, although Roy adores Cole. That might be a little tough for him, come to think of it. When the cancer was in its late stage, Cole took Roy's wife, Sandy, out on a surfboard." She crossed herself. "God rest her soul. It was one of her last wishes. To sit on a surfboard and watch the sunset."

Gulp. "*Cole* did that?"

Valerie didn't realize she would be running against a *saint*.

"He's such a sweetheart. An incurable flirt and it doesn't matter whether you're eighty or twenty-five. He just loves women. All of us, bless his heart. And everyone, both men and women, love him. But everyone loves you, too! And even more of them will once they get to you know again. Remember, you've been gone a while."

This was true. She hadn't been back to Charming for an entire summer since the summer after her high school graduation. And she wouldn't get to meet everyone at the Salty Dog. She had to get out and stop hanging out in the senior citizen trailer park as she'd done for most of the last six weeks.

"You should take some time and hang out on the Charming boardwalk. Meet the people."

"That's a good idea," Valerie said.

Gram stirred her coffee. "You know, you never told me what happened between you and Cole that last summer."

"Nothing. He joined the navy."

Joined the navy and blew up her plans. Valerie didn't have a gap year after all but had gone on to college at Mizzou. Met Greg Hill two years after graduation and married him two years later. She'd never heard from Cole in the intervening years. Then again, in true dramatic fashion like eighteen-year-olds everywhere, she'd declared that she never wanted to see him again.

"You know," Gram said, picking at her bacon. "Cole's father won that Mr. Charming contest several years in a row."

"Cole's father? But I thought Cole didn't know his father."

"After sweet Angela died—" She crossed herself again. "God rest her kind soul."

Valerie plunked down her coffee cup so suddenly that the liquid sloshed like turbulent waves. "Angela *died*?"

Why hadn't anyone mentioned this? Sure, she hadn't seen her in years, but Cole's mother had been one of Valerie's favorite people in the world. A teacher, she'd actually been an early inspiration for Valerie. The awful news slammed into her heart. She should have done a better job of keeping in touch with Angela, at least, if not her son.

Gram nodded sadly, bowing her head.

"W-when? How?"

"Let's see. Cole was overseas when she became ill. We all pitched in, of course, but the pancreatic cancer took her pretty quickly. Cole missed seeing her one last time but was given some kind of special leave from the navy for the funeral. I swear that poor boy looked like someone had torn his heart right out of his chest."

Oh, God. Poor Cole.

"Anyway, his father heard and got in touch then. Wanted to reconnect with Cole. Do you believe that he'd been living in Houston all this time? Lloyd. He bought the Salty Dog after he retired."

"And Cole bought *him* out?"

"More like rescued him."

Uh-oh. Valerie was fast becoming sympathetic to Cole Kinsella. Dangerous, that.

She spent the rest of her day off cleaning and

straightening, helping Gram with her physical therapy exercises, making lunch and dinner, and talking Gram into boxing up at least half of her Precious Moments figurines. They eventually settled on a third and Valerie called it a win.

At the end of the day, once Gram had been settled in bed, her walker nearby, Valerie poured a glass of Gram's cheap boxed wine and stepped outside.

The sun had ended its descent and she caught the tail end of its crimson dip. Nothing but a slice of dimming light appeared at the edge of the horizon. The lighthouse where Cole lived shone brightly and she wondered if he was home. She wondered whether he'd ever thought about her over the years as she had him.

Every now and then she'd look him up on social media but force herself away from the photos of him living his exciting life. To her, his life had seemed like one grand party. There were photos of him on a boat, hang gliding, surfing, at a bar with his buddies, always a beautiful woman or two nearby. He'd never been married. She'd followed him on Instagram once, then quickly unfollowed him, unable to take any more of the fun and carefree single life she'd assumed he was living. Just went to show how little of someone's real life was presented to the world on social media.

God knew her real life was different from what she showed. On her social media profiles she posted only joyful photos. Her college graduation, wedding day, anniversaries, parties and celebrations. Both the first and last days of school were chronicled yearly.

She didn't put up photos of the days when she had been too depressed to get out of bed, or selfies on the days when her hair hadn't been recently cut and styled. She didn't give status updates on the nights she cried herself to sleep because she didn't know how to fix her marriage. No pictures of the day she'd found out her husband had cheated on her.

Funny. Another thing that hadn't wound up on her IG account.

The rolling sound of the waves crashing pulled up a memory, sharp and clear.

Every summer since she was fifteen, she and Cole had taken up where they left off. If she'd had a boyfriend, and there'd never been anyone serious, she dropped him when she came to Charming. It must have been the same for Cole, because one way or another, he was always hers for the summer. There had never been any question. To everyone they knew, they'd be Vallie and Collie—but only she could call him that—joined at the hip every single breathtaking summer.

Foolishly, that last summer, she'd made plans for their future together. He seemed to be fully on board with her ideas every time she'd mention it after one of their heavy make-out sessions. They'd both graduated from high school that summer, and they'd planned to take time off. A gap year. She'd worked and studied for years and just wanted a break. They were going to drive to California where they'd live together and find jobs.

He'd surf the rogue waves and she'd take photos until she figured out what to do with her life after she finished college. She never thought about making a living with her photos, because that seemed like such a long shot. Her parents were less than thrilled. As a thirty-two-year-old, she now recognized the naivete of her "plan," which was more of a dream. But Cole, driven and ambitious, had known exactly what he wanted to do with his life. It would have been nice if he'd clued her in.

She'd seen Cole for the last time on this very same beach. His honey-colored hair, usually surfer-style long, was shockingly short and cropped. High and tight.

He'd joined the navy. They'd had a huge argument—their first, as she recalled, one of the few benefits of being only summer lovers.

"We had a plan!" she'd shouted above the cacophony of waves.

"That's not a plan. Hope is not a plan."

"Cole, the United States Navy is going to own you."

"This is what I want." His blue eyes met hers. "It's what I've always wanted."

"I thought you wanted me," she whined. "I thought you wanted us."

"Not like this. Not when I can't take care of you, not when I can't even support myself. I can't do that surfing. That's just not going to happen."

"I don't need you to take care of me. We were both going to get jobs!"

"Where? Which fast-food place? I'm not qualified to do anything but surf. The navy is going to be my education."

That had been the last time Valerie attempted anything bold or impulsive. The last time she'd tried to indulge in a dream. She'd returned to Missouri, put her camera away, and stuck to the familiar and the safe. Mostly, it had worked. Even after marrying Greg, she'd never fully depended on him.

Cole and her summers in Charming had represented the dream she'd imagined. But Greg had turned out to be the disappointing and harsh reality.

Ironically enough, Valerie had become a teacher not just due to Angela's influence, but because it was a practical way for someone who loved books to make a reliable living and determine her own financial security. She'd long ago come to accept that photography would be a great career for someone who wanted to struggle financially, and that dream of hers now lay somewhere between death and life support.

She'd been so stupid and naive. She'd felt so close to Cole whenever they'd been together, but she'd only spent a few summers with him. It hadn't been much longer before she understood that Cole had been right. About everything. By then it was too late to apologize.

Seemed now that she owed him more than her sympathies for Angela's passing.

Chapter Six

Cole and Max were relaxing in the living room of Cole's converted lighthouse. The beam of light still went on automatically, making him feel like a beacon at times. There remained something oddly comforting about the thought that he might still be a light for some errant sailor or hapless civilian.

The house had been remodeled to include a small but fully equipped kitchen, a guest half bath and a large living room. Upstairs, he had two bedrooms and a full bathroom, and an outer deck with a view. It suited his needs and he loved living right on the edge of the water.

Sub lay on his back, legs spread, doing a good imitation of roadkill.

"For God's sake," Max said. "Why don't you have him neutered?"

"He is neutered. Listen. We need to plan an event for this stupid contest, so let's figure something out."

Max took a pull of his cold beer and set it down, grimacing. "You got yourself into this mess. I said I'd applied for some grants. What do *you* do? Jump the gun."

"This is ten thousand dollars, free and clear, too. And we won't be at the mercy of anyone deciding whether or not we get their grant."

"You should have known something like this always has strings attached."

"This could get us a lot of publicity. Our new waitress is running, too."

Max chuckled. "For Mr. Charming?"

"Yep, she's a firecracker. It was all her idea. Guess she needs the money. But damn, so do I."

"Yeah, you do. We do."

When Cole bought the bar from Lloyd, he'd asked Max to come in as his partner. Frankly, Cole would have never gone into this business venture without Max. A brother in arms, Max had always been gifted when it came to finances.

"And who is this new waitress you hired?"

"Valerie Villanueva."

Max straightened. "You don't mean *the* Valerie you used to talk about."

"That's the one." Cole kicked back on the couch, splaying his hands behind his neck.

"The summer fling."

"Not a fling, dude."

"Yeah, right. I always thought she sounded too good to be true. You'd have every summer together and then she would leave? So you were a free man all year, but you had this hot woman waiting for you every summer."

"No, you were right. It *was* too good to be true."

That last summer she'd wanted more. What had felt like a lifetime commitment to him and would take him away from his goals. He'd wanted out of Charming, too, but he'd planned to go a lot farther than California. He wanted to see the world. He wanted steady work and a good future so he could send money home to his mother. A teacher, she'd always lived paycheck to paycheck in Charming. So he'd upset Valerie's plans and hurt her. Never saw her again. Until now.

"And she's running against you. This ought to be fun."

"Not so much. Valerie is gorgeous, so she's got that going for her. She's sweet and smart. The customers love her. She's a third grade teacher who's taking care of her grandmother."

"She sounds like a saint. Got the sympathy vote all wrapped up, plus the male vote. If you're not careful she's going to take away the female vote, too. You better kick the flirting up a notch or two. Make sure every woman thinks she has a chance with you."

"Why stop there? Maybe I should single-handedly

court every woman in town. Dinners, flowers, candy. Sure, why not?" Cole pretended to stick a knife in his chest.

"Hey, take one for the team." Max seemed to be enjoying himself too much. "C'mon, dude. You're a natural flirt. Just do your thing and you'll win. You have a good reputation here. And Valerie was a summer person. I bet half the town doesn't even know who she is."

"True. But I'm still tryin' to live down being Lloyd Kinsella's son. He used to win this contest every year," Cole muttered.

"What did *he* do for an event?"

"The event thing is something new. Ava's idea to put her mark on the contest this year. Apparently, it's not enough to have a woman running as Mr. Charming for the first time."

"Why don't you ask Valerie for her input? I have to believe that a teacher would have some suggestions. I bet she's had to put on a lot of events in the past."

"That's a good idea."

"See? I'm good for something."

He'd get Valerie to help. After all, they were in this together now, thanks to her.

The next morning, Cole parked at his usual favorite spot on the beach, and as he and Sub walked toward the swells carrying his surfboard, he noticed flyers on the parked cars. Curious, he pulled one off and there in black-and-white was a photo of Valerie, looking perky and adorable on what appeared to be the first day of school with her young students.

> *Hi, I'm Valerie Villanueva, and I'm running for Mr. Charming!*
> *I'm a schoolteacher from Missouri, and I used to spend summers here with my grand-mother! Now I'm back in Charming for an-other wonderful summer! I'm working as a waitress at the Salty Dog and I'd love to meet you! Come by for a drink or burger and I'll in-troduce myself and tell you why I think it's time for a woman to be Mr. Charming.*

"Gee, Vallie, did we forget an exclamation point? After all, shouldn't we end with one?"

Despite the fact that these flyers would proba-bly bring more business to the Salty Dog, he was mildly irritated. She was already way ahead of him and he never liked for *anyone* to be ahead of him. He crumpled up the piece of paper and tried to enjoy the waves for a couple of hours before work.

When he arrived at the boardwalk as the store-fronts were opening for the day, he saw Valerie in the distance. Dressed in a short white dress and sandals, this time talking to a family as if she'd met her new best friends. She caught his eye, called his name and ran to catch up to him.

Sub nearly wagged his tail off as she bent to pet him. "Who's a good boy? Huh? Is that you?"

Cole nudged his chin toward the family, setting up their umbrella for a day on the beach. "Nice work, Vallie."

"Cole," she said, and her gaze was soft. "I'm so sorry about your mom. I…I didn't know."

It felt as if someone had stung his chest with a poison dart, like it did every time anyone mentioned his mother. "It was a long time ago."

"I always liked Angela."

"She loved you."

She bit her lower lip, nodding, dark eyes glimmering with a suspicious wetness. "I've got to apologize for something else, too."

"What did you do? Wrap up this contest before we even got started?" He winked. Force of habit.

"I'm serious. You remember *young* Valerie. Vallie." She held up air quotes. "The girl with no real plan that last summer. I wanted to have an adventure with you. That's not me anymore. It didn't take long before I got my good sense back. You were right. And I'm sorry for my, uh, overreaction."

Well, damn. He hadn't expected for her to lead with, of all things, an apology.

"You want to apologize for having a dream?"

She gazed at him from under lowered lashes. "You know what I mean."

What he did know didn't matter now. But if he'd been in a seaside town in California, instead of a remote undisclosed location training for a rigorous SEAL mission, he might have been able to say one last goodbye to his sick mother. But no, he'd wanted to see the world, believing that everything else would stay the same and be ready for him when he returned.

"We were *both* young."

She winked. "Okay. So glad you're going to give me a pass on my youthful indiscretion, sweetheart."

"There she is."

She was back to her flirty self, practically batting her eyelashes. It appeared no one would be left standing in the wake of her magnetism, him included. Fine. He'd have to up his game.

"You're on the schedule for tonight," he reminded her.

"I'll see you then, boss!" She turned, a whole stack of flyers in her hands. "Right now, I've got people to meet."

"I want to talk to you about something later." He cleared his throat. "We've got to have an event. I need your help. You probably know a lot about this sort of thing."

"Because I'm a woman?" She gazed at him from narrowed eyes.

"Because you're a *teacher*."

"Oh. Of course. Sure, boss."

"Also? Stop calling me boss."

With that, he turned and went on his way.

Chapter Seven

Valerie met a lot of people on the boardwalk, and even though most of them had no idea what she was talking about, those who were actually Charming residents agreed to vote for her once she explained. She hadn't stopped to think that many of these folks had simply driven to the beach for the day and might not even live in town.

As she headed back to the boardwalk later that afternoon, plugging along in the Oldsmobile, she decided to stop in and introduce herself to some of the vendors on her way into work. She'd looked at the Mr. Charming list of entrants, and there was only one other vendor on the boardwalk participating. He worked for the Lazy Mazy Kettle Corn place, so she'd stay away from there. The place was dangerous to her health anyway.

Scooping up more of her flyers, she stopped at the saltwater taffy shop. Since Gram's love for peppermint would help keep them in business this summer, she hoped they'd offer her their support.

"Hey, there! I'm Valerie. You've probably seen me here before. My grandmother loves your peppermint taffy."

"How nice," the gentleman said, spreading both arms wide on the counter. "I'm Harry. What can I do for you, darlin'?"

"I'm so glad you asked! Well, you can get me a pound of the peppermint and also maybe you can vote for me as Mr. Charming?" She batted her eyelashes. Tossed her hair. Prayed for her soul.

He hooked a thumb to his chest. "You're talkin' to Mr. Charming three years runnin' here. Decided to give someone else a chance."

"Oh, my! You'll have to tell me all your secrets."

"No secrets. I'm just friendly. And people love my saltwater taffy." He nudged his chin in the direction of the old-fashioned taffy-pulling machine he kept going in the front.

It wasn't until that moment that Valerie realized he'd deflected. Probably another good friend of Cole's. Well, she wasn't going to be able to win everyone over.

"They must love you, too, surely." Valerie cleared her throat.

In any other town but Charming, she'd feel a tad uncomfortable. Harry had a ring on his finger, and she wasn't flirting with him, for God's sake. Just being friendly. Outgoing. But that did seem to work much better at the Salty Dog, where people tended to expect it from their waitress and realized it didn't mean anything.

"So, any advice for me?" She asked as Harry went to work shoveling peppermint taffy in a bag.

"Just keep doin' what you're doin'. I hear you're the best waitress the Salty Dog may have ever had. But…face it, sweetheart, you've got some stiff competition this year."

"I know. From my boss."

"And Tanner."

"Tanner?"

He snorted. "God's gift to women, don't ya know. He works at the Lazy Mazy Kettle Corn place down the way and just turned twenty-one. That makes him eligible to enter."

So that was the Lazy Mazy entry. Judging by Harry's attitude, at least he wouldn't be voting for Tanner. But if he was "God's gift," then perhaps all of the women would.

The ones not voting for Cole, that is.

Okay, deep breaths. I'm nice. Debbie will vote for me.

"You're voting for Cole, I take it?"

"It's too soon to tell. Though I will say that I'm silently rootin' for him from the sidelines. Cole's a good man." He weighed the bag and grinned, as it appeared to be right on the ounce. "One pound. Exactly."

"Oh, hey, you're good at that."

"Been doing this for years now. Finally got the hang of it." He handed it over and took her cash.

"Nice to meet you," Valerie said and slid the taffy into her tote bag.

She continued to walk down the boardwalk, noting the children lined up for the Ferris wheel. Valerie had been on this same Ferris wheel exactly once when she'd been ten. When it stopped at the top for what seemed like forever, her legs dangling helplessly from what felt like hundreds of feet in the air, she'd sworn she'd never get on it again. Even Cole had never been able to talk her into it and he had serious persuasion skills. A child squealed and she looked up to see the fools who rode the sky glider from one end of the pier to the other. Those molded plastic seats being held up by cables surely couldn't hold up anyone over 100 pounds.

She passed the Lazy Mazy, peeked inside but didn't see anyone who looked young enough to be him. She was now rather curious about this Tanner kid. Finally, she reached the Salty Dog. Sub sat outside, wearing a cute little getup. A T-shirt of some kind. Valerie wondered why he would be parked there when he usually hung out in the back office. As she got closer, she realized exactly why. The big bold letters on the back of his salivating bulldog T-shirt read:

Vote for My Owner, He's Running for Mr. Charming!

She bent to pet him. "You have a smart owner. I'd have done the same. You're both a chick *and* voter magnet."

Wondering if she should get a dog and park him outside, too, she walked inside. The early dinner crowd already out, the place was mobbed tonight. The aroma of burgers, fries and steak wafted through the air. Laughter and talking, bottled beers clinking, silverware clanking. Good for Cole. Business had been hopping every shift that she'd worked.

Valerie went to the back and found Debbie. "Tag, you're it!"

"My feet have never been happier to see someone." Debbie flung her apron off. "It's been a busy day."

"I can see that." Valerie pulled the Salty Dog tee out of her bag and slipped it on, then reached for her apron. "I saw Sub out front."

"Pretty funny, right? It was Ava's idea."

"*Ava's* idea?"

"Yeah, well, we've all seen your flyers, sugar."

"Hmph. It just seems like Ava should be impartial in this."

"Don't worry, she's not allowed to vote. If that were the case, I'd tell you to drop out right now. You wouldn't have a prayer. She's got it bad for Cole."

"I noticed that."

Valerie got busy taking orders and chatting it up with the locals. When she had her first order for a round of beers, she had a chance to check in with Cole.

"Nice job on Sub, by the way. If I wasn't running against you, I'd vote for you, too."

He winked as he slid a draft beer on the bar. "You like that, huh? Ava's idea."

"I heard." Feeling a little uncomfortable at the pinch in her stomach, she smiled through it. "Is she giving you a lot of good ideas like that?"

"I have some of my own."

"Speaking of which, when did you want to talk about planning the event?" She'd been kicking it over in her head since the moment Ava had mentioned it, and already had some ideas.

"Tonight okay?"

"Sure." Her drinks ready, she got back to hustling.

Tips were improving as the evening wore on. Her cheeks hurt from smiling almost as much as her feet did from standing. She'd forgotten it took a while to break in her waitressing legs.

"Y'all come again, please. Hope you had a great time," Valerie said as she dropped the check at a party of eight.

"Best service ever!" one of the men called out in Cole's direction.

"She's a keeper," Cole said with a nod and a wink.

Valerie flitted about tables, making sure to never

fail to be her charming self. Her party of one at table ten was an older gentleman whose keys she'd be taking before he left. He looked to be somewhere between fifty and sixty, nice-looking with a full head of gray hair. He'd had a liquid dinner, but she'd say one thing about him. He was a great tipper.

"How are we doin' here, sweetheart?" Valerie asked, praying he'd ask for food instead of another cold beer.

He held up a single finger. "One more for the road."

The smile froze on her face, but she hesitated only a moment. "Coming right up."

Valerie put the order in with Cole. "We need to do something about the gentleman at table ten. He's not driving. Take his keys or I will."

"I've got this," Cole said and went back to crushing ice and flirting with the ladies.

When Valerie set the drink down, she did so with a smile. "You sure I can't get you anything to eat? We've got great burgers."

"Nah, that's fine."

"This is your last one. If you need a ride home, just let one of us here know. We'll get you fixed up in a jiffy."

"Aren't you sweet," he slurred.

This made the first time since she'd started working here that a customer got this wasted. But at a bar, it had been bound to happen eventually. Despite the fact that "fun" might as well be her middle name tonight, she would wrestle the keys out of the man's hands if she had to.

As the evening wore on, the crowd began to thin as customers left, but the gray-haired man still sat at the table. Alone. Valerie felt horrible ignoring him, but she had said that was his last drink. He'd refused food and now the kitchen had closed. Besides, he had laid his head over folded arms on the table as if catching a snooze. Valerie tried to meet Cole's eyes, a tough thing to do, because he was behind the bar flirting with three women at once. She could only hope they were all tourists.

"Bye, Cole," one of them said, with a little finger wave. "You've got this Mr. Charming title in the bag. I'm going home to vote right now."

"Thanks, sweetheart." He winked.

Valerie snorted and joined Cole at the bar. "Shows what she knows. She can't vote until voting is open."

He simply flashed her that devastating grin, dimples flashing. "I'm sure she'll figure it out."

"Is that...was that your girlfriend?"

It hadn't occurred to her that Cole had a girlfriend or might possibly be engaged to a local. If that were the case, she'd sincerely have to up her game. Because that woman would have friends, and her friends would have friends. And so on.

"Why, you jealous?"

"That's funny. No, I just like to know where I stand."

He blinked.

"In this *contest*! Where I stand in this contest. What my odds are."

"And you think *your* odds would be worse if I *had* a girlfriend?" He chuckled. "I like my odds just fine now."

"Oh, great. So you're going to let every one of these women think they might have a chance with you just to get their vote?"

"I'm free and single. Every woman *does* have a chance with me." He slid her an easy smile.

Far more affected by his smile than she wanted to be, she hooked her thumb toward Wasted Dude. "You're still taking care of this?"

"Said I would." He came out from behind the bar and headed to his office, presumably for his keys, and Sub, who'd been led to the back after sunset.

Valerie said goodbye to the last of the customers, took off her apron and clocked out. She said her goodbyes and grabbed her bag, thinking she'd read a bit while she waited to talk to Cole about their event.

"C'mon. Let's get you home, Lloyd," Cole said to Wasted Dude.

Lloyd.

"Okay, thanks, buddy. I'm sorry if I drank too much. I just…that nice waitress… I…" he continued to slur.

Cole half carried, half held up his father as he walked him out the door, Sub following. This was Cole's *father*. Now that she knew, Valerie caught a passing resemblance. They were both tall, with the same strong and square jawline. But Cole favored his mother far more, with her blue eyes, honey-colored hair and beautiful, dimpled smile.

Poor Cole. Valerie was personally acquainted with fathers who disappointed, but this seemed to be a low that she couldn't wrap her mind around. Her heart seemed to be thudding in her chest like a wild animal trapped in a cage. She pulled her thoughts back to the event. Yes, the *event*. Focus. She had to help plan this. After all, Cole wasn't her only competition. Together, they had an advantage because they had a large area to throw an event. And a place where people could come and drink.

Drinks on the house? No. She shot that idea down immediately. Too expensive.

Although…maybe happy hour with drinks half price. Costume party? Come as your favorite character from a literary novel. Or a graphic comic book. Come as your favorite Star Wars character? No, thanks. She wasn't going to dress up like Princess Leia with the rolls on her hair.

She kept going, brainstorming every idea that had ever been suggested by her classroom's party committee or the Home & School Club.

Anything to avoid thinking about Cole taking his drunk father home.

Chapter Eight

Valerie continued to scribble ideas down on the back of one of her flyers as one by one the staff left.

Nick, the cook, was the last to leave. "Hey, need a ride?"

"I'm actually waitin' for Cole to come back."

He quirked a brow.

"We need to plan an event for this Mr. Charming contest."

"Ah," he said. "Happy planning."

Then he was out the door, leaving Valerie alone. Suddenly cavernous, the empty restaurant felt like a big, gaping hole. The quiet surrounded her and she heard every sound outside. A stray wrapper pushed along by the breeze. The crashing waves. Couples talking softly as they walked past the storefront, holding hands.

An hour later, she wondered what she'd do if Cole didn't come back tonight. She couldn't just leave the restaurant *unlocked*. The tightness in her throat made breathing difficult and she tried her relaxation exercises. The ones her therapist had recommended after the divorce.

"You tried your best, honey," her mother had said. "But when a man is unfaithful, he's the one who's broken the vows. You have nothing to feel guilty about. You loved him and he betrayed you."

But it wasn't quite that simple. Valerie had entered her marriage hoping for the best. Eyes wide-open, she swore she'd never marry a cheater. She honestly would have never expected that from Greg. He was supposed to be her safe choice. The man she'd wound up with because she didn't take chances anymore.

The door swung open and Cole strode inside. Here was a man who'd represented risk. He always stirred something crazy inside her. Wild. Her emotions always snapped and crackled with him. They ran the gamut. Those feelings of excitement collided and mixed with terrible uncertainty and were uncomfortable and overwhelming.

And she'd forgotten what it felt like…to be completely alone with him.

He slid in the chair opposite hers. "Sorry that took so long."

"Sub?"

"I swung by and left him home. He's had enough of this place for today."

"I'm sorry," she said. "You could have said something. I didn't know that man was your father."

"Now you do. It's fine. He occasionally comes in, drinks too much, needs a ride."

"That...doesn't sounds fine."

"Maybe not, but it is what it is. Right? Just so you know, I always take his keys." He gave her a quick smile, not flirty. Just...there.

His normally bright blue eyes dimmed, his lids hooded. Her heart gave a powerful tug.

"I didn't know that you had found your father until my grandmother told me recently."

"More like he found me. He showed up after I got out of the navy. Looked me up, said how proud he was of my service." Cole scoffed. "He wanted to make it all up to me, blah-blah. But as you can see, he's the one who needs a keeper."

"Oh, Cole."

"Okay. What do we have here?" The master of distraction turned over the flyer where she'd scribbled down her ideas. "Speakeasy? As in the days of the Prohibition?"

"Not one of my best ideas, but there's so much we can do with that."

"On the other hand, I'm kind of fond of the Star Wars idea. You in a Princess Leia costume would fulfill some of my teenage fantasies. Not a moment too late."

Charming and flirty Cole was back. The man who didn't let her, or possibly anyone else, see too deeply inside. It made her wonder if he shut down for everyone, or just her.

"Not one of my favorites. That was me just spitballing ideas."

He quirked a brow. "Spitballing."

"Maybe I've been around third graders for too long. You know what I mean. Those are ideas you throw up on a wall to see if they'll stick. Like spaghetti."

"Now you're talkin'. I love spaghetti."

"I remember."

Fondly, she recalled many dinners with Cole and Angela. They'd help Angela with the dishes, then settle down to watch TV while holding hands. Good times. Of course, that last summer they'd done a whole lot more than hold hands. Best not to think about that right now.

"What do you think of this for a flyer?"

Cole studied the paper seriously, brow creased, but then flashed her an easy smile. "Maybe one less exclamation point."

"Oh, you're one of *those*," she said.

Had he moved closer, or had she?

"One of what?"

"An exclamation point minimalist."

His lips twitched with a smile. "That's me. Exclamation points are for special occasions. Like Christmas Day."

"Let me tell you, buddy, an exclamation point is the best way to show your enthusiasm!"

"Too many, and it sounds like you're shouting all the time!"

"Okay," Valerie said, unable to hold back a chuckle. "One less exclamation point."

"Email this to me and I'll get some printed and hire someone to put them out. I'll upload to all our social media pages."

"You do that?"

"Yeah, no big deal."

"You manage the bar you also own, work as the bartender and keep up with a social media presence? Do you handle everything?"

"Hell, no. We hire someone to clean. And Max fills in as a bartender so I can occasionally have a day off. He also handles anything that involves a spreadsheet. Believe me, we're both slammed with work. But I'll get this done."

They discussed some of her ideas for the event, and how much it might cost to implement them. As she suspected, drinks on the house were out of the question, but Cole didn't even think he could swing a half-price happy hour.

He pulled out his phone and began swiping. "I'm on a strict budget. We need to streamline this."

Curious about his life, she asked a question that had been on her mind. "How did you meet Max?"

"We went through SEAL training together. He saved my butt a couple of times."

Her jaw gaped. "You're a navy SEAL?"

"Was."

"I knew you were ambitious, but I didn't expect that."

Nor had such a distinction shown up on any of his social media accounts. But it made sense he'd keep that private from those that didn't know him in real life.

"So, what event do you want to go with from these?" He handed over the paper after having crossed out most of her ideas.

Left uncrossed on her paper were only the Star Wars theme party and the speakeasy. She sighed. "Let's go with the speakeasy."

"Well, that didn't go as planned. Or hoped." He crossed his arms and grinned.

"Your first mistake was giving me a choice."

There was a moment between them that sparked with energy. They locked gazes, his eyes shimmering from under those ridiculously long lashes. Cole had always been a classic pretty boy, but the years had been more than kind to him. Beyond handsome, now he looked *interesting*.

His eyes occasionally contained a glint and hard edge to them that might have appeared frightening on anyone without those dimples. A small scar above his left cheek kept him from being too pretty. With broad shoulders, powerful forearms and the hint of a tattoo peeking from under his sleeve, he appeared to be someone that would command respect. Demand it.

"It's *never* a mistake to give you a choice, Vallie."

She cleared her throat. "Um, so, do you think maybe we could just have a contest? Like a costume contest, and the person who wins gets half-price drinks for…let's say a month?"

He squinted. "Two weeks. Sorry to be a tightwad, but Max might just have *my* ass for this. It's a no-brainer to me, because I'm going to win this thing, but Max isn't as certain."

"That's fine." She scribbled something down, then looked at the time. Nearly midnight. She found herself unable to suppress a yawn.

Cole smiled. "Hey, I'm sorry to keep you so late."

"If you don't mind, I'll finish this up myself."

"Mind? I'd give you my firstborn if you'll take care of it." He grinned and stood. "Now let me walk you out."

Cole locked up, pulling the iron gate across. A few decades ago, a devastating category two hurricane had blown through Galveston wreaking havoc, taking some of Charming with it, too. Cole had no illusions that the iron gate protected from that, and he considered water to be his biggest threat. Not criminals.

He did sometimes wonder how he'd been talked into buying a business this close to the water. The seawall helped. But it was one thing to live here and quite another to invest your life savings. The fault lay with Lloyd. His sad father, who now that he didn't own a bar, didn't have a woman, either. And Lloyd lived for women and booze. How he'd wound up with *his* mother, a saint, Cole would never know. Then again, Lloyd had a reputation for being quite…charming.

Sue him, but he was rather sick of that word.

Valerie stood behind him. Waiting. He studied her, her long brown hair blowing in the breeze, and a beat of silence passed between them.

"Okay, then. Good night," she said and began walking toward the now nearly empty parking lot.

He followed her, just to keep her safe, he told himself. She approached an Oldsmobile wagon. "This is yours?"

"Don't laugh." But her lips were twitching with the start of a smile. "I ride with the angels."

"Of course you do."

She unlocked the driver's-side door and threw her bag inside. "See you tomorrow."

He gripped the door frame, which definitely got her attention as her gaze slid up from his forearms to his eyes.

"You seeing anyone back home?"

If she thought it too personal a question, she'd tell him so. But he'd told her about Lloyd tonight simply because she'd asked, and he did not talk to anyone about his father. Cole continually swung between embarrassment over his old man and compassion for him. It couldn't be easy to wind up alone at sixty-five, with no retirement plan, and no one who seemed to care. He'd lost his former good looks, lost the bar and, never having married, had nothing to offer a woman anymore. Or so he believed.

"No."

Oddly reminiscent, though he'd never asked her before. Every summer she came back to him, as if she'd just gone to the store. They'd just pick up where they'd left off and there were never any questions about anyone else. For him, there had been no one else. No one quite like her. They'd had the kind of off-the-charts chemistry that now, as a full-grown man, he realized was rare.

Her hand slid down his arm, still planted on the door frame. She met his gaze, eyes soft. Warm. "Cole, I'm really sorry about your father."

"It's okay."

"No, it's not. You don't deserve this."

"I don't know that anyone does."

"And even if I'm going to beat you until you don't know what hit you, remember that you're *not* my enemy." As if to prove it, her hand squeezed his arm, and she leaned forward to kiss his cheek.

No other girl but his Valerie could make heat curl inside of him with a simple kiss on the cheek. Practically an air kiss, that one.

"You better get on home. Before I don't *let* you go home."

"Sounds intriguing." She got behind the wheel. "But you're right. I should get home."

Let me take you home.

"See you tomorrow," he said instead.

Chapter Nine

Two nights later, the night of the kickoff event arrived and the line went out the door.

Valerie had thrown together an outfit from secondhand store finds and Gram's closet. She looked like a saloon girl. Sort of. Debbie, who had opted out of dress-up, had written in white chalk on the wall directly behind the bar:

Get your giggle water here.
Juice joint!
Come for the hooch, stay for the fun.
Hello, Dolls! and
Have a roaring good time!

Debbie, a talented artist, had drawn pictures of vintage liquor bottles, and a man who looked like Al

Capone. They'd lowered the lighting inside to give the establishment the ambience of a gangster hangout. Max stood outside dressed like a 1920s hoodlum, head to toe in black, letting people in a few at a time. And Cole… His costume might be the best of all. He wore a long-sleeved white shirt with armbands around the sleeves, a vest and a white apron. In addition to looking like a Tombstone, Arizona, barkeep, he seemed to be getting into character. His usual flirting was dialed to extreme mode and he kept calling women "babe" and "dollface."

With every term of endearment, Valerie got in more of a snit. But she reminded herself this was a show and it wasn't only Cole performing. She had to pull out all the stops tonight when she had everyone's attention. Nothing could make this smile falter. Nothing.

Max led another group inside to be seated, and Valerie ran to welcome Mr. Finch and Lois. She'd invited all the senior citizens to attend but hadn't expected them.

"Oh my gosh, you two! I'm so glad to see you." She hugged both of them and seated them at one of her tables.

"I couldn't let Lois drive alone," Mr. Finch said. "I care too much about the residents of Charming."

"Honey, I can't drive once it gets dark," Lois said.

"Correct. A stop sign isn't a suggestion," Mr. Finch added.

"I thought you weren't coming. I'm so glad you're here."

"Don't you look cute," Lois said, appraising her outfit.

"I dug some stuff out of Gram's closet."

"And don't worry, she's fine," Lois said. "I got Etta May to come over and sit with her."

Of course, Gram insisted she was fine every night, but Valerie did like to get someone to stop in and at least check in on her once a night. Usually that was Lois as she lived closest.

"What can I get for y'all?"

Valerie got their orders, and then her next customers'. Every time she went to the bar to place a drink order, she heard Cole pulling out all the stops.

"Don't you look gorgeous, dollface. Any gangster would kill for you… If I wasn't wanted in three states, I'd definitely ask you out… Why, sure, I do agree he should have sent you flowers for an apology. I know I would have sent four dozen…"

It went on and on.

Then Ava walked in, dressed like a flapper girl, and holy wow, did she fit the part. Her straight blond hair was cut chin length, which suited the whole look. The black frilly dress was tight, especially around her tiny rump, and Valerie caught Max unashamedly checking out her ass as she strutted inside. She walked right up to the end of the bar where Valerie waited for her cocktail order.

"Isn't this just wonderful!" Ava said. "You two have really outdone yourself."

"Thank you, Ava," Valerie said. "We wanted this to be special."

"Cole said it was your idea."

"Well…it was *one* of my ideas."

She held her arms out wide. "No one else will come close to this."

"What's everyone else doin' for an event?" Valerie asked.

"Tanner is outside the Lazy Mazy right now with a sign around his neck that says, Kisses for Votes. Lame!"

Cole, who'd had his back to them as he crushed ice in the blender, turned around and snorted. "Yeah, Tanner."

As the evening progressed, Valerie slung drinks and carried out hot plates of food. So many of their regulars came out, but there were more people that she hadn't met. She took the opportunity to say hello to everyone she could, even those at the other waitresses' tables. About half of the customers had chosen to participate in the costume giveaway—there were flappers, though none as gorgeous as Ava, Al Capone–style gangsters and, of course, cowboys. *Mostly* cowboys. Valerie wasn't certain that could even be called a costume in Texas.

Growing a bit tired of all her peppiness because, darn it all, she shouldn't have worn these boots, costume or not, Valerie headed to her table where a man sat alone, his back to her.

"Hey, there! Welcome to our speakeasy. What can I—"

And then she stopped talking because she had to be seeing things. Maybe from the dim lighting that she wasn't accustomed to. A trick of the shadows.

"Valerie," said Greg.

"Um, hi?" Valerie said, because "Get out of here, you horrible piece of vermin" didn't sound polite. But, oh, Lord, how she wanted to say it.

"I guess you're surprised to see me."

"Well…"

"This felt like something that shouldn't be done on the phone. Your colleague told me you'd come back to Charming for the summer. And I saw your flyer."

Valerie ground her teeth and smiled. "You should have called."

"Not surprised to find you running back to Charming. Did you manage to hook up with your summer lover?"

"Why are you here?"

"Mr. Charming? Really?"

"Shut up, Greg," she said through a frozen smile. People were watching her, some of them catching her eye, waving goodbye and good luck. Valerie waved back.

"What can I get for you?"

The show must go on!

"I'll have a domestic beer."

At the bar, she placed her order with Cole, barely containing her hostility. There were nothing but women seated on the stools. And likely not one of them would vote for Valerie.

"Domestic beer!" she shouted.

He blinked. "What's wrong?"

Obviously being sweet all the time had cost her. A little anger and frustration seeping out were now too startling. Too shocking. Stupid Mr. Charming contest.

"I'm tired."

"Then why do you look like you're about to bite my head off?"

"Wow, I can't help it if you're *so* sensitive that you'll take a little bit of exhaustion and make it personal."

"Shh," Cole said.

"Oh, hell, no, you did *not* just shush me."

"Uh-oh," Ava said from behind Valerie. "Are you two okay?"

Valerie whipped around, dialed back to delightful mode, batting her eyelashes. "Of course. I get along just fine with the barkeep. Why, he keeps all those nasty gangsters away with the baseball bat he keeps behind the bar."

"She's a liar," Cole said. "It's a rifle."

"You two are hilarious. Love the script. Hey, I brought along the photographer for a photo of the two best Mr. Charming entrants," Ava said. "How about you come around here, Cole, and we can get a quick shot?"

"Gosh, Ava, I've got customers. I'm slammed—" Valerie said.

But Cole came around from behind the bar and threw his arm around Valerie. He tugged her in so close and tight that she got another whiff of his beachy warm scent. Her legs felt a little like wet noodles. His strong arm was low on her back, nice and firm. This made it the second time they'd touched. Look at her, keeping count. Two or three flashes went off and Valerie blinked.

"Did you see the mayor's here?" Ava said after the photo op was complete.

"No, I didn't." Valerie's throat tightened like a vise. "How nice."

Now she understood exactly what chicken felt like in a pressure cooker.

She delivered Greg's beer, then went back to her customers, engaging, appealing and being delightful to the nth degree. Martha Stewart had nothing on her. She chatted, flirted with a couple of college-age guys, checked on Mr. Finch and Lois, and kept busy until she could no longer avoid Greg's empty bottle and hateful glares.

"Can I get you another?" Valerie said, taking the empty bottle.

"That's the guy, right?" Greg nudged his chin in the direction of the bar. "The summer lover."

"Is this why you flew all the way here? Are you out of your mind?"

"No, but you must be if you're going after a guy like him. He's been flirting all night long."

"Shut up, Greg."

"You shut up. I always thought you were reasonable. Logical. But to come out here and try to rekindle something with your teenage lover...you're *thirty-two*, Valerie. Get real."

"My grandmother lives here," she said through gritted teeth. "The one you never liked me to visit?"

"That's a convenient excuse. You don't need to be gone all summer. I see what you're doing here, and it's really sad."

"What? What am I doing here?"

"You're trying to make me jealous."

At this ridiculous statement, it was hard not to throw back her head and cackle like a crazed witch. Nothing could be farther from the truth.

"Let's try to be civil. Are you going to tell me why you're here, or not?"

"I'm not selling the house."

It felt like a building had just landed on her. All the breath left her body. He couldn't mean that. They'd had plans. He'd finally promised to sell. Two *years*. She'd waited and fought him for two years to get her half of the home where she'd lived so miserably with him.

"Why not?"

"I'll have to buy you out. Regina claims it's in a good school district."

"I don't care. You've stalled too long. And you've proved that you can't afford to buy me out. Selling the house was part of our divorce agreement. Y-you can't do this." Her voice shook even as she tried to keep it light.

"My new lawyer said that happens all the time. I'll get financing and buy you out."

She'd heard that before. "It wasn't the deal!"

"Things change. You have a good paying job with the school district. I won't be unreasonable, and I'll agree to a mutually chosen appraiser for the value."

"Greg, your *photo* is next to the word 'unreasonable' in the dictionary. You can't just change a divorce settlement without a court order."

"Excuse me, Valerie?" said another customer nearby. "Could we get another round here?"

"I'll be there in just a jiffy, sugar!" Valerie's hand tightened around the empty beer bottle to the point she thought it might shatter, leaving her with a bloody stump.

"You'll have to take me back to court, then." He stood, fishing a few bills out of his wallet and tossing them down. "I think that would be even more expensive but have it your way."

Then he walked away, as always with the smooth gait of someone with a stick up his butt. How had she *ever* been remotely attracted to this man who was so mean-spirited and *vile*? She must have been in a coma when she married him! Valerie pasted on a grin, knowing she should leave any second now or risk committing homicide in a room full of people. Not the best way to get away with it.

Valerie went to the table waiting and took their orders, her hand shaking. For the rest of the evening, she counted the minutes until she could go home and let loose. She wanted to scream. She wanted to cry. She wanted to order a fresh drink just to throw it in Greg's smug face. She wanted to slap him until she got some *real* color in those pale cheeks.

Instead, she had to smile and flirt. She had to chat away like someone hadn't taken a mallet and smashed up her plans. She'd counted on that money to start over, even some to help Gram. A loan and financing would take him more time. Time he and Regina would continue to live in *Valerie's* house.

Finally, thank you, God, the winner of the costume contest was selected. Conveniently for Cole's finances, the winner was Abbie, known to Valerie as a teetotaler, and also dressed in a flapper costume.

"I'm so excited!" Abbie jumped up and down. "Is this half-off on drinks good for Diet Coke, too?"

"Absolutely, sweetheart," Cole said with a wink.

"Let's thank our wonderful hosts for such a great kickoff event. Don't forget voting starts tomorrow and will be open for two weeks. You can vote online, or just fill out the form we have at the Chamber of Commerce. I've got some here tonight if needed." Ava waved the forms in her hand.

A few people grabbed them, some grinning at Valerie and pointing to the form, winking as they left. She smiled back, hanging in the back near the bar. The scream in her throat was still fresh and Valerie didn't know if she'd make it to her car.

"What's wrong, Vallie?" Cole said from behind the bar. His voice was soft. Kind.

"I...I need to go." She threw off her apron. "Would you clock me out?"

If she didn't leave now, she would blow up like the Fourth of July. And she'd leave litter and sparklers everywhere.

"Yeah. Everything okay?"

"No." With that, she flew out the door.

Chapter Ten

If Cole wasn't mistaken, Valerie's eyes had been shimmering with a suspicious wetness before she whipped out of the bar like she had a Tasmanian devil on her heels. Didn't make sense. All their plans had gone off without a hitch tonight. The serendipity of having a Diet Coke fan win the half-off on drinks couldn't be planned.

Tonight, Valerie looked somewhere between a saloon girl and his teenage fantasies. That red dress was…doing stuff to him. There was a slit on the side that went up fairly high on her leg and every time she moved a certain way, he saw bare skin tapering down to sexy, kick-ass black boots. He'd been practically drooling for hours.

He should probably let her go, but he couldn't. The way she'd run out of here wasn't right. All night she'd flirted, laughed while serving drinks and burgers. He must have missed something.

"Be right back," Cole said to Max, who had started to count the till with something close to a smile on his face. And Max didn't smile.

Valerie stood outside, head bent, arms crossed, pacing, muttering to herself. "I can't believe it. I can't believe it."

"What can't you believe?"

She blinked, surprised, and maybe a bit alarmed, to see him there. "I'm about to scream. You'll want to stay back three feet because I can be loud."

"Baby, I don't scare easily."

"I mean it, Cole!" She tossed her hands up. "I thought I could wait, but I can't. And if I scream in the trailer park, someone will call 911. Quiet hour starts at eight."

"This may sound like a dumb question, but why do you have to scream?"

And then, with zero further warning, Valerie Villanueva's face became as red as a stop sign, and she shrieked. A loud wail with no words. She was right.

She could be loud.

And he was at her side in half a second, tugging her into his arms. She didn't resist, but practically crumpled into them.

"I'm sorry. I've wanted to scream like that for two years."

"*What* in the living hell? Was that a caterwaul?" Max appeared at the entrance.

"Nothing," Cole said, waving him back inside. "I've got this."

Valerie had curled her hands into fists at his chest. Her breaths were coming short and shallow, no doubt from all the oxygen she'd expended on that hellacious scream. He slid his hand up and down her spine in a soothing motion.

"I c-can take a lot of stuff, really I can. I handled my parents' divorce, my grandmother's stroke and the divorce from my cheating ex-husband. But I can't take this. It's asking too much."

Cheating ex-husband. That was news to him. "At the risk of repeating myself, what *happened* tonight?"

Valerie didn't answer but dissolved into heart-wrenching sobs. Her body heaved against his and it seemed that she would fall if he didn't hold her up. He half carried, half dragged her into his office, not caring if anyone noticed. Sub rose from his bed and wagged his tail, certain that would solve everything. One hand gesture from Cole and he sat back down again with a heavy sigh. Sub couldn't solve all problems.

Cole firmly shut the door to his office with his back while Valerie continued to sob in his arms like the world had ended.

His heart raced so fast that he feared he'd stroke out any minute.

"Please, Vallie, tell me whose ass I have to kick. I'm dying here."

She kept her face buried in his neck. Tears wet his shirt collar, his neck, and he didn't give a shit about any of it. He just wanted the sobbing to stop, and he wanted the name of the person who'd caused it. Because someone had done this, and he only hoped it hadn't been the ex. He simply stood there, back against the door, arms around her waist, holding her tight against him. Moving closer to his desk to grab a tissue, he handed it to her, and let her get back to the sobbing.

She clutched that tissue in her fist and when her sobs slowed to heartbreaking hiccups, he led her to his office chair and slowly sat her down on his lap.

"What happened to you, baby? Let me fix it. Please let me."

She dabbed at her eyes and her nose. "You… c-can't."

"I can try." He tucked a random stray hair behind her ear.

"I wish…you could." She spoke between hiccups of breaths. "No one can fix this. My ex was here tonight. Sat at my table and I…had to wait on him and pretend I didn't want to kill him. Because, you know, I'm so *charming*."

At this, he jerked back, and his spine stiffened to granite. "You should have said something."

"Like what?"

"Like 'Get someone else to wait on him. I can't do it.'"

"He wouldn't have let up. What he wanted to do was tell me how he's trying to ruin my life again."

All the breath left his body. As he'd suspected, Valerie was in trouble. Her life was far from perfect, far from the carefree and always smiling woman he'd seen the past week.

Max knocked on the door to the office and popped his head in. "Leaving now. Everyone's clocked out. Lock up."

Cole simply nodded and Max, eyebrow quirked, shut the door.

Valerie, who had hidden her face in the crook of his neck when Max walked in, pulled back and met his gaze. She dabbed at her eye with the tissue and then looked away. He saw something in her gaze shift, and it was almost as if she'd made the decision to shut him out. Again.

"Tell me." He tugged on her hand, wanting the connection.

"I shouldn't have fallen apart like this. It's no big deal, just another obstacle, but I'll get through this one, too." She sniffed. "We had an agreement to sell our house and split the profits. It was part of our divorce, and a court order. Now he shows up tonight to tell me he's not selling, and he wants to buy me out. He and his new girlfriend want the school district."

Cole rose, taking them both up. He took Valerie's hand and led her outside the office to the bar, where he stepped behind and rummaged around for his favorite bottle of scotch. Expensive and smooth, he'd first opened this bottle the day of his mother's funeral. When things seemed so dark that he thought he'd never get on the other side of his grief.

He plopped it on the bar. "A bottle for when things get particularly rough."

"But what will you have?" She took a seat on the stool.

He plopped two shot glasses on the bar and poured. "Been there, done that. Bought the T-shirt."

"Here's to bad times," Valerie said, holding up her shot glass.

"And good friends to get you through them."

They slammed them back. The scotch was the smoothest he'd ever tasted, and went down easy.

This couldn't be the reason Valerie had entered the contest, but he found himself wanting to drop out so that she could use the money and take the worm back to court.

"Don't you even think about it." She studied him from under hooded lids, almost as if she'd heard his thoughts.

"You need this money now more than ever."

"Don't worry. It's just…this couldn't have come at a worse time. I'd counted on that money to…help get me through this summer."

"Need a raise?" He poured another shot. "Although, I have to believe you're raking in the tips."

"I am," she said with a wink.

Interesting. And yet, it wasn't enough.

There's something you're still not telling me, sweetheart.

He'd leave that for another day.

All the makeup she'd had on her eyelashes had smeared off, making her intoxicating dark eyes pop out. He'd never seen more beautiful eyes. When he'd complimented them once, she'd laughed, and said they were double *B*s: brown and boring. But since her, he'd noticed other brown eyes, and none were like Valerie's. Hers shimmered with humor and intelligence.

"Are you really done with him?"

She laughed and almost snorted. "Oh, hell, yes," she said and met his gaze. "For about two years. He was a mistake."

"Why did you marry him?"

He'd been curious from the moment he'd heard about this man. This man who'd had something Cole had once wanted for himself: Valerie in his life 24/7 so he could kiss her anytime he wanted.

"Yay, we're starting with the easy questions." She plunked down her glass and nudged her chin for him to fill it.

He did, but not one for himself. Someone would have to drive her home tonight.

"Greg was the safe choice. You've heard of a safety school in case you don't get into the college you want? I give you Greg Hill. I know, I'm a sad case. But for a long time, that's all I wanted. Security.

And…I thought I loved him enough. He obviously got the memo that I didn't, even before I realized it myself." She slammed back the shot. "What about you? Did you ever get married? Engaged?"

"I was engaged once," Cole said, and Valerie jerked her head back in mock surprise. "Hey, don't give me that look. I can do commitment."

"And what happened?"

He shrugged it off because he'd tired of reliving this story. In some ways, Jessica had reminded him of Valerie. But there had been something pretty basic missing. When he'd met Jessica, he'd been vulnerable. Lonely. She'd filled a need for the sense of family he'd wanted but when that hadn't worked out, he realized something true.

"We weren't right for each other."

She narrowed her eyes. "Did you cheat on her?"

He met her gaze. "I'd never *cheat*."

She smiled, already three sheets to the wind. "Good, because why does anyone cheat? You know? Why not just say, look, I'm done with you. Let's end this."

He put the bottle away and she didn't seem to notice. "I think maybe people cheat because they don't have enough courage to say those words."

"Maybe I didn't have enough courage, but I didn't cheat. My vows meant something to me."

"Didn't have enough courage for what?"

"To end the marriage," she said.

"You? Not enough courage? You don't believe that. Tell me you don't believe that."

"I can't do that. I won't lie to you. I've never lied to you and I'm not going to start now," Valerie said, and then nearly fell off the stool. "Oopsie."

She would have fallen had he not caught her. "Easy there, Vallie. I think it's time to drive you home. I seem to have forgotten you're a lightweight."

Her hands came flush against his chest and she smiled up at him. "Would you do that? That's so nice of you. I haven't been nice enough to you ever since this stupid contest started. I get too competitive. *That's* going to change, buddy. Because you're a prince."

"I wouldn't go that far."

"Yes, go that far. Absolutely."

She studied his eyes, and an incredibly intimate moment passed between them. A moment in which he remembered the way she tasted.

"Did I ever tell you that I love your dimples?"

"You may have said something a time or two." He grinned, brazenly taking his advantage.

She cupped his chin. "Please don't ever get rid of them."

"I don't think I could if I wanted to."

"They're so sexy," she said, thumping his shoulder, a buddy movement not at all in tune with her words, which were hitting him in unexpected places. "*You're* sexy."

"Okay," he chuckled. "Back at ya."

"Aw, thanks." She pulled out of his arms. "Well, I should probably go home now."

"We should both go."

She walked a few steps and turned to him. "Except...I need a ride."

"You sure do, and I'm your man."

He walked behind her, shutting off lights, locking doors. She swayed a bit but overall seemed to manage walking. Just not so much in a straight line.

Outside, he opened the passenger door to his truck and offered his hand for a lift.

"A prince." She took his hand and climbed inside. "Woodland Estates Mobile Home Park, please, driver."

She hadn't buckled yet, so he reached over to do it for her, then went around and strapped himself in.

He drove toward the park where he had always assumed his mother would eventually live. Many of her lifelong friends were there now. People like Roy Finch, who'd lost the love of his life. When her last wish was to watch the sunset on a surfboard, Cole had made that happen. And even though Roy was six foot five, and about as tough a man as they came, he'd cried like a baby after his wife died.

Cole hadn't cried over his mother's death. Not in years. He figured he'd have to schedule that in at some point, but for now, it stayed back in the special compartment he'd built for "regrets."

And there it would stay.

"This is the one." Valerie pointed as he drove at

the five-miles-per-hour speed limit posted for the park. "Gram will be asleep by now. The entire park folds up by eight."

Every mobile home they passed had the lights out. "I'm going to walk you to the door."

"You don't have to do that."

He pulled over and turned to her. "I'm going to walk you to the door."

"You're annoying." She put a hand to her forehead. "Oh my gosh, I'm worried I'm not going to remember any of this tomorrow."

"I'll remind you." He winked and came around to the passenger side.

When he opened the door, she was struggling with her seat belt. "I'm stuck."

"You're not stuck." He reached across her lap to help and damn it all...she *was* stuck. "Okay, so you're stuck."

"What's wrong with your truck?"

"Nothing's wrong. This is a new truck."

"I *never* get stuck in the station wagon."

"That's because you ride with angels." His head was practically in her lap and wasn't this a lovely place to be. He jiggled and pressed and found the problem. "I think your, um, lace is caught."

"Don't rip me!" She tugged at it and then burst into laughter.

He finally must have jiggled in the right way and her seat belt unclicked.

Finally free, she turned her body. For a long beat

they simply stared at each other without words. She ended the silence when she fell out of the truck and right into his arms. He couldn't have planned it any better had he spent weeks strategizing this moment.

"Hey, there." She smiled up at him. "Good catch."

"You're welcome."

"Cole?" She tilted her head and gave him a heart-tugging smile. "Don't tell anybody. But I think I'm a little infatuated with you."

He ran his hand through her wild hair, which for once had been down tonight.

"But you shouldn't let that go to your head."

"I won't." He traced the soft curve of her jawline and his heart pounded like a wild animal bucking against its cage.

He reminded himself to calm down because the alcohol had lowered her inhibitions. The ex showing up tonight made her vulnerable. And he would not take advantage. But when her hands threaded through his hair it was hard not to groan.

He'd somehow been waiting for this moment a long time. To feel this much for someone again. To allow himself to care. To be invested. His own defenses were down for the count, but not because of alcohol. This was 100 percent Valerie. He'd missed the connection that had always taken him a bit by surprise.

"I always loved your long hair," Valerie said softly. "It killed me to see you, of all people, with a military buzz cut. The first thing I noticed when

I saw you again was that you looked like you had every summer. I missed you."

"I missed you, too."

"And I always, always thought about you."

The words hit him like a sledgehammer. He'd of course thought of her, too, over the years, always pushing the memories away because he hadn't deserved her. And when she'd said that she never wanted to see him again, he'd taken it to heart, never quite getting over the fact that he'd done what he had to do even if it meant losing her.

"I didn't mean to get you this drunk, baby." He brought her hand to his lips and kissed it. "I should have stopped you."

"No, that was all my doing. You meant well. It accomplished what I wanted. To forget the worst time of my life and focus on the best times. Which are ahead of me. I know exactly what I'm doing right now."

"So do I. You're getting inside your grandmother's house without tripping once, and you're going to go inside and get to bed."

She gave him a pout and lowered her arms to his neck. "That's what I'm going to do, but it's not what I want."

"That makes two of us."

They weren't a good idea, this wasn't a good idea, because she would leave again at the end of the summer. And he was sick of temporary. Sick to death of being left behind. But at the moment he didn't much care. He dipped his head the short distance to meet her lips. Not a tender kiss, as he met her sweet warm tongue. Hand on the nape of her neck, he tugged her even closer, just drinking her in. Wanting more. She responded, telling him she wanted this. She wanted him.

He pulled away first, gratified to leave her a little breathless.

"Get some rest and if you need my special hangover recipe? Call."

Chapter Eleven

The next morning, Valerie woke to the rattling sound of the air-conditioning unit in her bedroom. Her head was the size of a bowling ball and felt too big to be held up by her weak neck. A horrible taste in her mouth reminded her far too much of what it might feel like to lick a city bus seat.

Sitting up, she cradled her enormous head. "Oh, boy."

Stupid, stupid, stupid.

She'd *kissed* Cole last night. Unfortunately, she remembered that.

Sure, Val, go ahead and throw yourself at the man. Do everything but a striptease in the parking lot of the Salty Dog. Perhaps some orange cones and a big neon flashing arrow pointing to you would complete the ensemble.

Me! Me! Sleep with me, Cole!

She made it to the bathroom just in time to get sick. Reaching for a rag, she wet it and held it to her forehead, then slid down the wall. She still wore her boots, so obviously she'd simply collapsed in bed. *And* she still wore her saloon girl outfit. Fantastic. So yeah, she'd had too much scotch last night.

And oh, dear Lord, had she really professed her undying love for him last night? No, *no.* Okay, she hadn't confessed love, just…her infatuation. Yeah, *so* much better. Damn her efficient memory cells! And damn alcohol for being too much like a truth serum.

Because she'd wound up kissing Cole. A little unprofessional of her, but hey, he would only temporarily be her boss, so it didn't count. Oh, wow. Delusion could be a wonderful thing. Oh, my, the way he'd looked dressed in his barkeep outfit. Yum. At one point he'd rolled up the sleeves of his shirt to his forearms that were corded with sinewy muscles. She actually didn't blame anyone who voted for Cole in this ridiculous contest because she half wanted to vote for him herself.

Mr. Charming. It fit him.

She would apologize to him today for kissing him, running her fingers through his hair and using him like a big, handsome, sturdy walker. She didn't drink anymore, that was the problem. But if ever there had been a time and occasion to slam back some good scotch, it had been last night.

She'd screamed like an out-of-control insane person! Cole had blinked. Twice. Max had given her a stern look that said he had no doubt that his new waitress was 100 percent certifiable. But hey, she'd held back that scream for two years. It was a wonder she hadn't ruined her vocal cords. Greg was still interfering, still controlling her in the only way he could.

After showering and changing, Valerie walked to the kitchen where Gram sat at the table, eating a box of cereal, her walker parked nearby. She'd made a lot of progress in the past few weeks, getting around the house on her own.

"I'm sorry," Valerie said, grabbing a cup of coffee. She'd be mainlining as it might be the only thing she could manage to keep down. "I overslept."

She shoved the cereal box in Valerie's direction. Froot Loops, for her daily fruit servings. Valerie's stomach lurched.

"No, thanks."

"How did the event go? Did you see Lois and Roy?"

"I did. It was nice of them to come out."

"They're voting for you. I think even Roy might be."

"Are you sure?"

"Well, Lois can be pretty persuasive." Gram elbowed Valerie. "I don't know if you noticed, but they seem to be having some kind of a...relationship."

"No, I hadn't." But it struck her as pretty sweet that Mr. Finch would even consider taking a chance on love again. "Did you vote yet? Voting is officially open."

"You know how I am with the computer. I'm not going to spend my time registering to vote if they ask me for a password and then it doesn't work. Then I have to spend an hour getting a new password. Besides, I don't like feeling like an idiot because I can't tell if that little square is part of a traffic light."

Valerie brought her laptop to the table. She navigated to the Charming, Texas, Chamber of Commerce website and found the link to the Mr. Charming contest. All of the contestants had been listed just last week, but now she only saw three: herself, Cole and Tanner.

"This isn't right. Where are all the other contestants?"

She scrolled but saw no one else listed. It hardly seemed possible that in the week since she'd last checked everyone else had dropped out. The voting would stay open for a couple of weeks to insure that even those on vacation without internet access would have a chance to vote.

"How beautiful!" Gram pointed to the photo taken of Valerie and Cole at last night's event.

My, my, someone was quite efficient at updating their website. She was going to point the finger at Ava. That woman was a whirlwind. Valerie just couldn't help liking her. In her, she saw a kindred spirit. Except that Ava was likely peppy all the time while Valerie… She struggled some days.

"We took this photo last night."

Before the evening had taken a dive, she'd flashed her flirty smile into the camera, head cocked. And Cole… He appeared to be looking at her instead of the camera. His eyes were hooded, his smile almost… surprised. As if he half hadn't expected to see her there. Heat pulsed through her and seemed to radiate through her body. He still had that effect on her.

After showing Gram how to vote, Valerie excused herself. She told a little white lie that she had an errand to run. This was true, of course, but it would be a complicated errand. Once the dishes were rinsed in the sink and Gram was settled with a book, Valerie grabbed her tote bag and keys, and then remembered that she had no car. She'd have to walk and figure out how to get Gram's car back later.

She walked the short distance to the office near the entrance of the trailer park. The morning already approaching temps usually achieved only on the sun, she faced another long Texas summer day. Fortunately, the office was cooled to the point of near arctic freeze. Betty, a fortysomething woman with short salt-and-pepper hair, waited behind the desk. She actually wore a *sweater*.

Valerie's options to help Gram from her own funds had disappeared. Winning the contest wasn't a certain thing, much as she'd like to believe it, and though she'd talked to Betty over the phone many times she'd only met with her once.

"Hey, there, Valerie," Betty said, offering her hand. "How is Patsy doing? I hear from the residents who play bingo that she's made a turnaround."

"A lot better, thanks for asking."

Betty glanced at her computer screen. "You're here to discuss the space rental and back fees."

"I'm sure that we can get this all ironed out. The mobile home is fully paid for. My grandfather owned it outright."

Betty flipped through papers, her lips pursed together. "But there is the space rental and that's *quite* overdue."

"We've been chipping away at it. I still don't understand how you can kick my grandmother out of a home she owns."

"Oh, we have no intention of doing that." She flipped through more papers. She was an expert flipper.

"The notices she's been getting, they're so—"

"Those are probably from the corporation that recently bought the park." She stopped flipping. "They won't kick your grandmother out of her home, no, of course not."

"That's good to hear. The language in them is pretty litigious."

"They can't kick her out of her home. They can, however, force her to move her home."

"Um, *what*?"

"Yes, the space rental is the only thing this corporation owns. Land rights. The ability for your grandmother to park her home there. They own the land."

"That makes no sense at all. How can we move the home? It's not like it can be hooked up to a truck's hitch."

"No, but homes are moved all the time. Residents upgrade to a newer model or they take their existing home where they can find a better land lease. That's why they're called mobile homes."

Valerie bit back a snarky retort. *Really? Is that why?*

Betty frowned. "I know this must be an emotional time. If only Patsy had said something sooner, and not just ignored all the notices."

"She'd lost her husband. I know she shouldn't have ignored all the past-due notices, but my grandfather always took care of all the bills. And then the stroke happened. Everything just hit her all at once."

"I know, and I'm sorry. The best option, at this point, is to come up with the entire lump sum and stop this eviction process immediately."

"I'm trying. But that's an awful lot of money to come up with at one time."

"Sugar, if I were you? I'd get myself a lawyer."

It wasn't a bad idea. "Last I checked, they cost money."

Because of that catch-22, needing to hire and pay

an attorney to slow down the process of paying back
a lump sum of money, Valerie had respected Gram's
wishes. After all, her home would be sold, and she'd
get her half. It should have been imminent, according to Greg the liar.

Until now. *Now* she had no other options.

Outside, the humidity felt like someone had
thrown her under a hot, wet blanket. Thank goodness that the rain forecasted would reduce some of
the oppressive heat, at least for a little while. She
rummaged through her tote bag and found her phone.

He answered after the first ring. "Valerie?"

"Hey. We need to talk."

After his morning run at the waves, Cole left Sub
at home and stopped by Lloyd's because they were
due for a serious discussion.

They'd had a short one last week when Cole had
driven him home and put him to bed. But Cole was
done humoring his old man, taking time out of his
schedule to drive him home. Worrying whether
maybe there were some nights he drank at a bar out
of town. Houston or Galveston, maybe. Who would
take his keys away then? Would the old man get behind the wheel and hurt someone?

Cole was exhausted of being his keeper. Weary
of losing sleep wondering if Lloyd would get behind
the wheel of a car before Cole could do anything
about it. Sadly, it wasn't primarily his concern for

Lloyd that drove Cole, but concern for the safety of the public at large. Lloyd had a choice. Others in his path might not.

And Cole didn't owe Lloyd a thing. He hadn't taken on the bar and grill simply out of misguided loyalty for his deadbeat father. Cole was too smart for that, and even if he hadn't been, his best friend certainly was. Cole had only agreed to bail Lloyd out after he and Max had done their due diligence. The Salty Dog, according to Max, had once been a cash cow. And it could be again with smart management. Cole saw ownership as a chance to live full-time in his hometown. Max had been working at a tech firm in Austin at the time, well paid but unhappy. Cole had been working for an elite private security agency in Dallas and was burned out being muscle for the wealthy.

Life was simpler in a small town like Charming. Calm. And now, as if the universe wanted to further assure him that he'd made the right decision, he had Valerie, too. Well, he didn't *have* her. Yet. She'd always been a bit of an obsession for him. A good, healthy one, since it had been 1,000 percent reciprocated. Every summer since he'd met Valerie had been the same for him. His was a "Vallie summer" and he looked forward to that all year long like some looked forward to Christmas.

Cole rapped on the door to his father's condo and was almost knocked over by a woman throwing the door open.

Her short hair was white with pink highlights spiked into a fauxhawk. The rest of her outfit was equally colorful. Purple spandex tights and white knee-high boots.

"Hiya, sweetheart. Sorry about that. I'm in a hurry to catch my bus."

It was only then that Cole took a good long look at her and saw that she had to be sixty if a day.

"Is Lloyd inside?"

"Yes. We had a bit of a wild night, though, and I need to get back to my assisted living center before they figure out that I'm gone."

Assisted living center? Okay, so she had to be older than sixty. Maybe even older than sixty-five? It was hard to tell, and she certainly moved fast.

Waving goodbye, she called out, "Door's not locked."

At least Lloyd was seeing women his own age, and—please, Lord—he wasn't paying for companionship. At times like this, Cole appreciated that Lloyd had stayed out of his life until he was grown. Mom had given him an almost idyllic childhood with the kind of home where he could have friends over at any time. Unannounced. They'd lived in a small and modest home but his mom working as a teacher meant they knew everyone. And she made *everyone* feel welcome. She never gave up on anyone, even a seemingly lost cause.

She was the only reason Cole stood outside the door to Lloyd's condo, a bag of groceries in his arms.

Because, yes, he'd eventually forgiven Lloyd just as his mother had. Once a week, Cole dropped by to check in on the old man. As usual the dank, moldy odor in the apartment hit him hard. Closed curtains kept the light out. The air conditioner rattled like a locomotive train at full blast.

"Hey, son," Lloyd said from his BarcaLounger, where he seemed to be nursing a hangover. *And* a beer.

"Lloyd, what the hell?"

Cole still refused to call him Dad. His father hadn't earned that privilege. When, and if, the man ever grew up, Cole would rethink. There didn't seem to be any danger of that happening anytime soon.

Lloyd hung his head. "Sorry about the other night. Made a damn fool out of myself, I expect."

He set the bag of groceries on the kitchen counter. "Right now, I'm talkin' about the lady who just barreled out of here on her way to the bus."

"Mitzi? Oh, she's a good friend. What are you kids calling it? Friends with benis?"

Cole closed his eyes. "Please never say that word again."

"Aw, Mitzi and I go way back."

Cole swiftly removed the can of beer out of his father's grip. "Hope she makes it back to her center okay. Did you ever stop to think it might be irresponsible to keep her out all night? Why is she in there, anyway?"

Other than her choice of clothes, Cole didn't see anything wrong with her.

"Her family is overprotective." He waved dismissively. "She could live on her own, but they just worry too much. Have one kitchen fire after you're sixty-five and everyone thinks you've lost it. I had a kitchen fire when I was thirty-five. Did anyone care? Was I in danger of being committed? No. It's ageism, pure and simple."

Cole ignored that ridiculous comment, poured a glass of orange juice and handed it to his father. "We need to talk."

"Already said I'm sorry."

"It can't happen again. I'm done worrying about you. Done carrying you home stinkin' drunk. The next time, I'm calling the cops. I promise you."

"It won't happen again." He took a swallow of his orange juice and grimaced. "Not that this is any excuse, but I honestly don't know what to do with myself anymore."

"Take up a hobby."

"Maybe I could fill in at the bar for you sometime."

"No."

Lloyd sighed. "Heard you're runnin' for Mr. Charming. Isn't that a kick. You know I won for years, right?"

"No one has *hesitated* to remind me."

"I like that new waitress of yours. Didn't even get mad at me when I wouldn't order any food. She looked so worried I half expected her to bring me something to eat anyway. When she cut me off, it wasn't like when Debbie does. She was even sweet about that."

"Yeah, that's Valerie." Lloyd didn't know Cole's history with her, and he'd like to keep it that way. "She's also running for Mr. Charming."

"I heard about that." Lloyd chuckled. "That's sure going to make this year interestin'."

"Yeah, well, we have to make those improvements soon. The ones you kept putting off for years. We have a month to get something happening or they're going to shut us down."

"That won't happen."

"How do you know it's not going to happen? Max has been working on this, trying to get us more time. But no one's budging so far. So, if I win, we'll use the contest money for that."

"What do you mean *if* you win? You're a shoo-in!"

"*No* one should underestimate Valerie. It would be a huge mistake."

"She's not even a mister! Hey, it's a cute idea, and I appreciate it, but when it comes right down to it this contest has always been won by a man."

Cole could almost hear Valerie's voice: *well, maybe it's time to change that...*

But with $10,000 on the table, he *couldn't* just bow out. She would enjoy some good old-fashioned competition.

"Either way, if you drop by again, don't be drunk.

And don't sit at Valerie's table. She doesn't need you taking advantage of her compassion. Debbie is who *you* need."

Chapter Twelve

Cole headed back to Woodland Estates to get Valerie's key so he could drive her car back.

For a change, Max would be working a shift at the Salty Dog tonight. Because Cole sometimes felt like he lived there, and that wasn't too far from the truth. He figured this would be his life for the next few years until he and Max got this business going on autopilot. That was the five-year plan.

He pulled in front of the home where he'd dropped off Valerie and knocked on the front door.

It took a couple of minutes, but Mrs. Villanueva opened the door. "Come on in, sugar, you're lettin' all the bought air out."

She looked a little weaker than the last time he'd

seen her at the Piggly Wiggly but she still had that sweet smile and dark eyes that reminded him so much of Valerie.

"Hey, there, sweetheart. I'm sorry I haven't been by to wish you well since you got back from the hospital." He'd been at the hospital, of course, along with Mr. Finch, one of his mother's closest friends.

"That's all right, sugar. You're here now." She led him inside to the kitchen. "Valerie will be out in a minute. She had to take a shower. That girl took a *walk* today, can you imagine? Glory be, I'm surprised she didn't drop dead in this heat. She was, however, soaked to the bone with sweat. Young people. You think you're invincible."

"I guess we do." Hyperbole was something the good folks of Charming were heavily prone to and he'd become accustomed to it by now.

"Would you like a cold Coke?"

"Let me get that." Cole rose and took a couple of cold Cokes out of the fridge, handing one to Mrs. Villanueva.

Mrs. Villanueva took a seat. "I'm sorry about this Mr. Charming nonsense, honey. That contest should be yours to win. Sometimes I don't know what my Valerie is thinking. We don't need that money."

"I'm glad she entered. It's made this interesting."

"Really, it's not like her to do something this impulsive. She worked hard, got good grades at school, went on to college to become a teacher. She's made us all very proud."

Cole remembered more of the spontaneous side of Valerie. With him, she'd always been up for an adventure, and for trying something new. For taking a risk.

"Oh, you're here," Valerie said.

She'd appeared in the door frame of the kitchen, wearing a white sundress that hit just above the knee. Her long hair, still damp, fell loose around her shoulders. Her lips were rosy pink and she was barefoot. She was fresh-faced, with not a hint of makeup on her face, and appeared younger. His mind flashed back to that feisty eighteen-year-old that wanted to have a yearlong adventure with him. This wasn't the first time he regretted not taking her up on that.

He stood. "Hey."

They simply stared at each other for a beat, and Mrs. Villanueva broke the silence. "Cole dropped by. Isn't that nice."

"I need your keys."

There seemed to be some kind of internal struggle going on with Valerie, as she opened her mouth, then closed it, then opened it again. Cole was two seconds away from telling Mrs. Villanueva that her car hadn't started last night. A harmless lie.

"I drank a little too much last night and Cole drove me home."

Mrs. Villanueva sat up straighter and quirked both brows.

Obviously, the granddaughter she knew as only

conservative had surprised her. "Goodness gracious. Well, thank you, Cole. How kind."

"My pleasure."

"I'll get my shoes." Valerie toed on a pair of sandals by the front door, pulled her hair into a ponytail, and grabbed her bag and keys from a bowl by the front door. "Be back soon, Gram."

"Take your time." Mrs. Villanueva waved them away.

He held open the door for her, then did the same with the passenger door. Within seconds they were off.

"I'm sorry about last night. I really didn't mean to lose it the way I did."

"How much do you remember?"

"I remember everything. I wasn't that drunk." She touched her ponytail. "Why?"

"Just wonderin'." His lips twitched in a smile and yes, he was looking for a reaction.

"Why are you smiling like that? Stop it!"

"So…you don't remember when you jumped on the bar and tried to do a striptease for me?"

"*What*? Please, no. Did I… When did I…" She was nearly hyperventilating. "No, I don't *remember*."

"Neither do I, because it didn't happen."

She shoved his shoulder. "Aha. You think you're funny, do you?"

"I have been known to be."

"No more laughing. I had plans, you know? *Solid* plans. We've been arguing about that house for two years and Greg finally agreed to sell it this summer. Then he just changes his plans. Just like that."

"It's interesting that he'd fly out here to tell you that."

He'd found it more than a little curious. It seemed that conversation could easily be had over the phone. The only explanation was that Mr. Hill wanted to see Valerie in person.

"He's still trying to control the situation. And me."

"He never learned that the force of VV can't be contained?"

"No, he's not a smart man." She cleared her throat. "He never liked me visiting Charming. Jealous, I guess."

"Of your *grandparents*?"

"Of you."

He met her gaze, but then had to turn his attention back to the road. It gave him time to think. "Why me?"

"Because I'd told him about you."

"Yeah?"

"Cole, I need to be honest. I wrote down my name as Valerie Hill because I wanted you to think that I'd moved on."

"It worked."

"Not really, since I changed my mind about letting you think I was still married within five minutes of talking to you."

"You can't lie to me, that's all."

"Are you so sure?"

"Baby, you couldn't even lie to your grandmother about being drunk. I was ready to jump in and save you."

"No, you're right. I can't lie to her. I'm obviously not the girl you remember. I don't take adventures anymore. Zero risk."

"If it helps, I regret every day that I didn't take you up on that offer. One year wouldn't have made that big a difference."

The benefits of hindsight and maturity. He'd been too eager to start his military career, sheltered, stupid young and unaware of how much it would take from him. Not quite as much as it gave back, it had turned out.

"That's the last time I considered doing something crazy. I kind of miss the old Valerie. I used to be kind of fun, right?"

"You still are."

A moment later they were in the boardwalk's parking lot, the station wagon sitting in the same spot they'd left it. He pulled into the closest spot.

"I'm sorry I kissed you last night," she blurted out, turning her entire body toward him.

"If there's any apology needed it should come from me. I kissed *you*."

She squinted. "That's not how I remember it."

"Well, you'd had a little scotch."

"Hmm. I thought it was me."

"Out of curiosity, if you had kissed me, why would you apologize for that?"

"Because I sprang it on you. Here you were, trying to do a good thing, and I...I practically attacked you."

It was difficult not to smile. "*Attacked* me?"

"Look, I'm trying to apologize here. Just because we used to be together every summer that we were both single, that doesn't mean I can kiss you anytime I want. Drunk or not."

As she turned and reached for the car handle, he took her free wrist and yanked her toward him. She made a little sound in the back of her throat, but it wasn't nearly as gratifying as the one she made when he kissed her.

When he finally broke the kiss, she stared at him, lips bruised and pink.

"Now there's no argument."

A hint of a smile curving her lips, her tongue flicked out and almost absently licked her lower lip. It was his undoing. He tugged her by the nape of her neck and drank her in. She tasted exactly the way he'd remembered. Sweet, with the slightest hint of vanilla.

Then her hands were in his hair, and she moved even closer so that she was nearly in his lap. And Jesus, they were probably fogging up the windows now. He should stop the madness, but no. Not him. He wasn't stopping a damn thing.

But as was his luck lately, she broke the kiss, shaking her head slowly. "Funny. We're different people now, but this...still the same."

"Yeah," he said, pressing his forehead to hers. "I'm not surprised."

The sound of a family walking past them caught his attention, reminding him of where he was.

"I want to go on the roller coaster!" a little boy shouted.

"You threw up last time," the mother said.

They walked past his truck, their voices growing thinner as they went. Valerie bit back a smile. So did Cole. He was going to have a difficult time the rest of the day not smiling like a hyena, or some other animal that smiled a lot. He wound a lock of her hair around his finger, playing with the strands, not ready to let go of the contact. She'd always had that effect on him. Every summer, he'd wanted a little more. Just a bit longer.

"Cole... I'm...obviously very attracted to you still."

"I'm with you so far." He'd locked gazes with her, and this close, the moment felt intimate. "But..."

"I'm leaving at the end of summer."

"You're here now." He brushed a kiss across her knuckles.

A summer had always been enough. This time, there was actually the glimmer of possibility. A teacher who could work anywhere in the country. Last he checked they had schools in Charming.

"What are you doing later?" she asked.

"Why?" He narrowed his eyes.

His plans involved super important stuff like taking a nap, watching the game, catching up on email and a midnight surf if he got lucky. He rarely got a day off.

"Because there's another meeting of the Almost Dead Poets Society tonight and it would be nice if I had somewhere else to be. Like maybe a lighthouse?"

"I'll give you the tour. But first, you have to tell me something. What exactly *is* the Almost Dead Poets Society? Because you've mentioned this twice now."

Her cheeks pinked and she looked at him from under hooded eyes. "It's that place where my grandmother gets to recite erotic poetry about my grandfather. Or at least I think it's erotic. But she's my grandmother!"

He cringed a little. "I've definitely got to rescue you."

"I love them all, don't get me wrong, but the poetry…it's…um…really…*bad*."

"How bad are we talking?"

She made a face. "I think some of my third graders are better."

He let out a low whistle. "Girl, you've made your case."

"Okay, I'll see you tonight, then." She gave him a slow smile.

He watched her until she got in her granny car and drove away with a wave.

Chapter Thirteen

A light rain turned the day crisp and clear. Valerie rushed home and spent the rest of the day with Gram. Cleaning house, cooking and watching TV. She took advantage of the temporary reprieve from the sweltering heat and baked chocolate chip cookies in the air-conditioned kitchen.

"You remember that I can't stay for the whole meeting?"

"Too bad, honey, tonight my poem is *When We Walk in the Rain.*"

Walk and lord only knows what else.

The gang arrived on schedule and gathered around Gram, giving her hugs and asking about her physical therapy progress.

"Hi, Mr. Finch," Valerie said, hugging him a little tighter than normal. "How are you?"

He smiled, something Roy almost never did. "Fair to middlin'."

"As long as our knees are holding up, who's to complain? Right, Roy?" Susannah said as she walked in behind him and propped up her closed umbrella in a corner.

"Oh, my hip is killing me in this rain," said Lois. "Why can't they make rain-resistant hips? If we can put a man on Mars—"

"We have *not* put a man on Mars," Mr. Finch interrupted, the former aerospace engineer in him clearly irritated.

"I beg to differ," Lois sniffed. "I saw the movie."

"The one with Matt Damon?" Susannah said. "My, that young man is so handsome! So unrealistic, right? Have you ever seen an astronaut that looked like *that*?"

"I don't know," Lois said. "That Neil Armstrong... I wouldn't have kicked him out of my bed for eating crackers."

"Ladies, for goodness sake." Roy cleared his throat. "A little decorum."

Valerie was about to intervene with a plate of cookies when in walked Etta May. She had a man with her who did not appear to have yet reached senior citizen status.

"Everyone, meet my grandson, Jeffrey James Virgil VII!"

The *seventh*? Really, what were they, a dynasty? Because Etta May nearly pushed Valerie toward Jeffrey James, she wound up using the cookie platter as a barrier. "Cookie?"

"Why, I don't mind if I do," Jeffrey James said with a drawl indicative of the deep South.

"Do you, um, like poetry readings?" Valerie asked, silently hoping that he didn't because he would surely be disappointed tonight.

He wasn't bad-looking. Tall, dark, with a trim goatee. But this was clearly a fix-up and her temper burned.

"I'm very supportive of anything that my grandmother does. It's the Virgil family way." He took a cookie. "Do you participate?"

"No, please. I'm just the hostess."

"And she's running for Mr. Charming!" Lois clapped.

Susannah raised her hand. "Sugar, I saw one of your flyers at the Piggly Wiggly on a BMW. That man seemed so *angry* as he tore it off his windshield."

"If she wins, I'm going to talk her into going to one of those spas in Houston," Gram said.

"I don't expect your vote, Mr. Finch, and that's okay," Valerie said, waving it away. "Cole is also running, and I know how fond you are of him."

"He's such a good boy," Lois said. "Oh, how I miss Angela."

At that rather painful memory, there was a sudden stillness in the room. A sniffle or two. Gram, of course, crossed herself. Mr. Finch lowered his head.

"Anyway!" Etta May stood in the center of the room. "Let's turn our thoughts away from doom and gloom, and the big C, and hear from our laureates."

"Before you start, I'm sorry I'll miss you all tonight," Valerie said and then took only a moment to consider her next words.

She would have rather kept this news to herself, but she didn't want any more fix-ups like Jeffrey James. Well intentioned though they might be.

"I have a date tonight."

For a moment, gentle faces with aging eyes simply stared back at her as if they hadn't heard right.

"What did she say?" Susannah whispered to Lois.

"A *date*?" Gram said. "With...?"

"Sorry, Gram," Valerie said. "I meant to tell you earlier. But I...have a date with Cole."

There was a collective sigh from the women and Mr. Finch brightened considerably. Gram crossed herself and looked up at the ceiling with a smile. No need to ask for *her* approval, clearly.

"Well, well. How nice. Tell Cole I said hello," Mr. Finch said. "You'll miss my new poem, *Texas Is on Life Support*, but you'll catch it next time."

"I definitely will." Valerie nodded.

She felt a tiny pang of sympathy for Jeffrey James, who suddenly looked like a deer in the headlights, but hey, she'd been listening to these senior citizens' poems for weeks. Encouraging and supporting even when she cringed. He could deal with one night. The gang forced her into taking a plate of cookies for Cole, and nearly shoved her out the door minutes later. Valerie wasn't sure which of them, herself included, was more excited about this date.

Because she'd been entranced by the old lighthouse since she was a child. Fascinated by some of the historical fiction books she'd read with lighthouses, she'd let her imagination run, making up stories of lost sailors at sea. Of flashing beacons leading the way home. Some of the first photos she'd taken the summer she had a digital camera were of Charming's nonoperational lighthouse.

Now the beacon shone brightly in the distance, lighting up the warm coastal night for miles.

Taking a moment before she knocked on his door, she admired the regal fixture. A weather-beaten white with light blue trim. For the first time since arriving, she wished she'd brought her good camera along, but that had been sitting in the back of her closet for years. Instead, she took out her phone and snapped a few shots, unable to resist the composition of towering flashing light, beaming stars and moonlight.

Cole and Sub appeared at the front door. "Welcome to Sub's house. He lets me live here."

Cole wore a pair of blue board shorts low on his hips and a white short-sleeved cotton button-up…unbuttoned. Tantalizing tanned skin and sinewy muscles lay underneath.

Sub nearly wagged his tail off but was so well behaved that he didn't jump or try to sniff her in embarrassing places.

"Cookies." She handed a plate over to Cole, then bent to pet Sub. "Hey, Sub. Are we a good boy today? Huh? Huh? Are we?"

Sub panted that he'd indeed been a good boy, and could he please have some bacon? At least, that was what Valerie thought he'd said, but she was interpreting.

Cole took the plate, dimples flashing through the beard scruff on his cheeks and jawline.

Taking her hand, he led her inside. And Valerie stepped into a nautical world. There were portholes for windows, and moonlight streaming through in streaks. In the morning, she imagined, the sun would do the same, leaving random patches of rays here and there. She walked to one of the windows that gave her a breathtakingly beautiful view of the gulf. The floors—a teak wood—gleamed.

"This is it." Cole stood in the middle of the great room downstairs. "Kitchen, great room, bathroom that way. Upstairs, there are two bedrooms and a full bath."

Oh yes, the *stairs*. They were winding and led to a wraparound second-story landing with more porthole windows. It was…incredible.

He caught her gaze. "It's a recovered ship staircase."

"I feel sorry for you," she said. "You have to live here. Poor baby."

He slid her an easy smile, hands shoved in the pockets of his board shorts. "Don't get too excited. I'm a renter. Our esteemed mayor, Tippy Goodwill, owns this place. She put a lot of money into renovating it."

"I can see that."

Inches away from her, he smelled like hints of the wind, warm sand and coconut. He'd probably already been out on the waves today. Cole had a long-term love affair with the water. Swimming pool, lake, ocean. Boat, canoe, surfboard. Submarine.

She turned to him, not realizing he'd moved so close. They were practically bumping shoulders. He met her gaze and a quiet moment passed between them that felt thick with tension but somehow... sweet.

"Want a beer?"

Cole made his way to the kitchen, still carrying the plate of cookies. He set it down on the long granite bar that separated the kitchen from the living room.

"Sure," she said, wondering why she suddenly felt so awkward.

They hadn't had any trouble earlier today in his truck. Now she didn't know where to put her hands. This was only the third date she'd been on since becoming a single woman. And the first in which she'd actually wound up at the man's home.

It's okay. This is Cole.

Cole handed her an uncapped beer and she took a

seat on the couch. Sub quickly hopped up and made himself at home on one end. He glanced up briefly, then went back to snoozing.

"I don't think I've said so but thank you for taking a chance on me with this job." She took a pull of her beer. "Honestly, it was getting to where my only friends were from the senior citizens' trailer park. Don't get me wrong, they're great."

"Except for the poetry club."

"Except for that. I've already made friends with so many people because of the job. Ava is very nice. And Debbie's great."

He nodded. "Debbie hung in there with us when almost everyone else took off."

"What do you mean?"

"For some, job security is everything. I don't blame them. Because if we don't make the improvements the Historical Society wants us to make by next month, we might have to shut down."

"Shut *down*?"

Valerie's throat tightened. She'd never asked Cole why *he'd* entered the contest, simply assuming he'd wanted the notoriety. The attention. The extra cash that never hurt anyone. Never once had she stopped to think he might be in trouble, too. Guilt slammed through her.

"Don't worry about it. The contest isn't our only plan."

Short of slapping her forehead, she didn't have words. She was appalled at her own lack of sensitivity. Just because Gram was in trouble didn't mean that there weren't also many other people and places struggling.

She'd just never imagined it about the Salty Dog.

"I'm sorry. I wish I'd known. But I didn't know you guys were in trouble. Not like that. Businesses always need more money, but...this sounds different."

"I didn't tell you this to get your sympathy. You know about my father. It just felt like the right time to mention why we lost some of our help. Why I hired you. It wasn't just a favor. We needed you." Cole stood. "Hey, want to go out and see the deck upstairs?"

He held out his hand and after only a brief hesitation, she took it. The stupid tingle hit her once more when he didn't release her hand as they walked up the spiral staircase and then out to a short deck. She wasn't sure if she let go first or if he did, but suddenly she stood upstairs with both hands on the rail of the deck, facing the ocean. Here, the warm wind whipped her hair around. The scent of salt rose heavy in the air. Seagulls squawked nearby. She was suddenly one of those women she'd read about, searching the horizon for her lost love, on a boat and lost at sea.

"This is what I want to show you." His hand went around an old-fashioned telescope. The kind that had been used in an actual working lighthouse.

Her hand slid down the telescope. "Just when I

thought this place couldn't get any cooler, you hit me with this."

"Take a look." He beckoned her. "Sometimes, during the day, it's clear enough that you can see cruise ships in the distance. But tonight, you'll see plenty of stars."

With Cole directly behind her, she adjusted the lens and looked out on the vast ocean in the distance. The moonlight beam shone across the ocean, giving her a good view of the swelling waves as they rolled in from a distance and crashed on the rocks below. The stars twinkled, competing for top billing.

"Have you ever seen a shark through the lens?"

He chuckled, so close his breath tickled her neck. "Yeah, both through the scope and on my surfboard."

She whipped around and nearly butted noses with him. "Oh my gosh! While you're surfing?"

"Take it easy. Mostly bull sharks and tigers. They don't get very big around here. Nothing to worry about." Then he smoothed down her wild hair as if grateful for her concern. "This would make a great photo."

"You're probably right." But her phone would not do this breathtaking view justice.

"It's what you wanted to do with your life. Photojournalism."

"Just a silly dream."

Yet the entire reason she'd attended Mizzou. After a while, that career path had seemed impractical and she'd switched majors.

"No, it wasn't. You were talented."

She'd taken many a photo of him, her favorite subject. Both on a surfboard and off. One of them had won a contest. She'd given Angela and Cole the framed winning photo, a black-and-white shot of him as he walked toward the ocean carrying his board under one arm. She wondered if he still had it somewhere.

After that last summer she'd taken the safe route. Mom's experience, not to mention Cole's change of heart, had taught her never to depend on anyone else, and Valerie would support herself, thank you very much. Photography had been sidelined for years.

"It turned out to be nothing more than a hobby." She swallowed hard. Inevitably, Cole brought about sweet memories of a simpler time.

"Surfing is still just a hobby for me, but I get to enjoy it every day."

They were still inches away from each other and she'd forgotten the deep blue hue of his eyes. Unnerved, she bent her head and pressed against his shoulder. So familiar. Comforting. The tug of lust hit her hard when one hand went around her waist, then lowered to her hips. The other hand remained on her hair. Caressing. Holding. She wasn't going to lie. The closeness, his touch, were more than welcome. Memories flooded back, reminding her that not all memory cells were cruel. Those were some of the most precious times of her life.

She smiled, her heart flopping around in her chest like a fish. "I'm happy for you."

"Yeah? Why?"

"Because you have all this. You have good friends, a business, and you get to do it all from here."

"It's all right." Cole studied her mouth but made no move to kiss her. But both hands squeezed her hips, warm and tight around her, tugging her close.

She tilted her head up and kissed him, intending something sweet. Tender. But that changed quickly when Cole licked her bottom lip. At the same time his arms tightened, and he pulled her closer. A seagull squawked and the wind whipped her hair into a frenzy of waves, but she was only vaguely aware of this. Instead a sensation so foreign to her she almost didn't recognize it pulsed through her body, causing a sweet ache between her thighs. Lust and desire formed tendrils of heat as the kiss went on and she heard the soft sound of a moan. Hers.

She broke the kiss. "It seems like we can't just kiss, can we?"

"We are pretty explosive."

She wasn't going to sleep with him. She wanted to, but it just wasn't that easy. He'd been her first, and she'd fallen in love. Hard. He hadn't. That was okay, she understood; he'd been young. He'd had plans that didn't include her. Also okay. She shouldn't have assumed that her eighteen-year-old first lover would be with her for the rest of her life. That was the kind of stuff of fairy tales and romance novels.

Slowing herself down, she stopped studying his lips to meet his eyes. "I fell in love with you once, and I can't do that again."

His blue eyes flashed with an emotion she couldn't read, and he didn't say a word. Just listened.

"And I don't do sex without commitment."

She didn't read disappointment in his eyes. Once, she'd been able to decipher his every emotion, whether it be anger, lust, hurt, or pain. But adult Cole had changed. This man guarded his emotions. If he wasn't flirting and putting on a show, she had no clue what he was thinking. Even now.

He simply brought up her hand to his lips. "Okay. We'll just hang out, baby. I promise I'll keep my hands to myself."

"Well, you don't have to do *that*." With that she turned back to the ocean and linked his arms around her waist.

She pressed her back against him and gazed at the stars. He lowered his head to her shoulder and kissed her neck. And they stayed that way for a long time.

Chapter Fourteen

A few days later, a heavy rainstorm was predicted, and all boardwalk vendors were prepared. In south Texas, rain was never a soft and gentle pitter-patter. Instead, the drops sounded like angry bricks falling from the sky, and the wind kicked up, blowing away umbrellas, bicycles, and anything not nailed to the ground.

But the waves were particularly good right before a big storm, and Cole and Max took full advantage of them in the morning. Sub jumped through the waves as they rolled in, barking here and there when he saw a seagull. There weren't many today as they could read the weather.

"Did you check out the website yet? Half of the

contestants dropped out," Max said as they carried their boards out of the water. "I talked to Henry, the grocery store owner, and he says everyone has dropped out because they think it's either you or Valerie for the win."

"Even Tanner?"

"Not Tanner. He's still hanging in there."

"Of course he is."

"Honestly, just entering that contest was a lot of publicity we didn't have to pay for."

Entering Mr. Charming had given Cole a new perspective. He'd grown tired of being known as the town flirt. Tanner could go ahead and take Cole's unofficial title. He'd been gunning for it for a while, always trying to one-up Cole at every turn. No surprise he'd given out kisses for votes. Once, that might have been Cole.

But after his mother's death, he understood the importance of family more than ever. Her loss had kicked him in the teeth, and he realized how tired he was of being abandoned. He'd wanted family of his own, some unconditional love, but hadn't met the right woman. Then, his girlfriend, Jessica, had announced she was pregnant in their first six months of dating, and he'd been happy for about a month.

He'd proposed, and she'd accepted. Though he wasn't quite in love with Jessica, she'd be the mother of his child, which deserved his respect and commitment. He'd obviously liked her enough to sleep with her, so he'd grow to love her, and all that. Bottom line, he'd do the right thing by his child. Unlike his father, who'd cut and run.

But Jessica claimed to have had a miscarriage. However, her lack of emotion at the time over this enormous loss was incomprehensible to Cole. She'd wanted to move full speed ahead with their wedding day, not taking any time off to grieve, or physically heal. She'd recovered quickly, not requiring any medical care, but all the reading Cole had done suggested that wasn't the norm. All of his many questions were deflected, one after the other.

Cole realized then that either he was about to marry the coldest woman on earth, or he'd been a victim of the oldest trick in time.

Both were true. The question of whether she'd ever been pregnant at all signaled the end for them.

And he hadn't felt a damn thing for anyone since Valerie waltzed back into his life asking him for a job.

Once he'd situated Sub in the office later that morning, Cole went about the business of preparing for the rain. Never one to wait until the last minute, he also checked on everyone else.

"Ready for this storm?" he asked Karen.

"Do you have any extra sandbags if I need them?" she asked, worrying a fingernail.

"Gotcha covered." He waved. The seawall meant they likely wouldn't need them, but best to be prepared for any eventuality.

"Oh, thank you, Cole! You're a lifesaver. Do you think it's really going to be that bad?"

"Probably not, but you can't ever be too prepared, yeah?"

Cole even stopped by the Lazy Mazy, where Tanner was just opening up.

"Oh, hey, there, Cole. Did you see it's just you and me left in the running? I have a lot of people voting for me, so you know, good luck and all."

"Don't forget Valerie. She could kick both of our collective asses."

"Yeah," Tanner snorted. "Don't think so."

"Got sandbags?" Even before he'd asked, Cole knew the answer.

Tanner wouldn't accept help. He saw that as some kind of a weakness.

"No, we're good, man. I've got this."

"I'm sure you do." Cole gave him the thumbs-up and kept walking.

Maybe he'd have Valerie come by later and see whether she got a different answer out of Tanner.

Two nights ago, they'd spent the evening talking, knowing that more kissing would simply get them too revved up. He understood her concern and was shocked to find that he agreed. There wasn't anything attractive about casual sex for him anymore. He'd wanted the real thing for a long time. So he'd listened as Valerie caught him up on the last fourteen years of her life.

She'd never had that gap year and had gone to

Mizzou in the fall, about the time he'd finished basic training. After a year, she'd switched her major from journalism to a bachelor's degree in education. When she'd confessed that his mother had been an early in-spiration and role model, his gut pinched. Though he didn't like hearing that she'd given up on her dream career, it seemed she'd found her calling and he couldn't argue there.

For the next two nights, they'd spoken every night over the phone, or texted. She'd recited "Doodle, Doodle, You're My Little Poodle," Susannah's poem about her pet cockapoo, over the phone to him, which gave him a much-needed belly laugh when she used a nasally voice reminiscent of Julia Child. He liked having her in his life even as a friend and had forgot-ten how much she made him laugh. How she made him think.

When Valerie walked in for her shift around three, he'd just finished wiping the bar for the fifth time, and outside the skies had begun to darken. Both the sky and the ocean were the color of gunmetal, such that the horizon blended into one color. The rest of the afternoon the sky darkened further, and only a few regulars dropped in for a cold beer, or a burger and fries to go. On the beach, families arrived and then left early, packing up umbrellas and coolers sometimes within minutes of arriving. When Cole stepped out for a look, he saw that half of the ven-dors had shut down for the day. He should probably do the same.

He turned to the few stragglers. "Hey, everyone, pack it up and get on home. This storm is going to make driving home challenging in a few more minutes."

One by one, customers, then the kitchen staff, left, then Debbie, and finally Valerie brought up the rear.

"What about you? Aren't you going home?"

"Not me. Sub and I are stayin'."

"All *night*?"

"I've got a love seat in there. I'll stay until the worst of this storm passes. In case this roof caves, I need to be here."

With the improvements they already had to make for the Historical Society, Cole didn't need any more damage.

"That's ridiculous. I'm not leaving you here. What about *your* safety?"

"Vallie, I think I can handle a Texas thunderstorm. I've been through enough of them."

"But…"

"Stop acting like you care about me. I might let it go to my head." He winked.

The rain came down in earnest, all at once, and thunder crackled.

"You better get going before it gets really bad out there." He worried about her driving, but he'd never get Valerie to stay here with him. "Let's hurry. Need me to walk you out?"

"Are you kiddin' me? We have thunderstorms

in Missouri, too, you know. Even tornadoes pass through occasionally."

"We have *hurricanes* in Texas. You really don't want to see one of those."

"Are we really going to argue about which state has the worst weather?" She glanced at him once more, then outside to the rain, a bit uncertainly. "Okay, take care. I would really hate to lose you at this point."

"Why? You might actually win Mr. Charming if this storm carries me out to sea."

"I don't need the *storm* to win. I'm going to beat your butt fair and square."

"You really better go now before I worry about you driving." He hesitated. "You *did* bring an umbrella."

"Of course, I did." She bit her lower lip. "It's in the car."

He did a mock groan and reached behind the bar grabbing the umbrella he kept for forgetful customers. "Here you go."

"Thanks," she said, taking it a bit sheepishly. "I'll see you tomorrow. Just…please…stay alive."

He watched as she walked out into the rain, briefly resembling a monsoon at this point, until he couldn't see her anymore when she turned toward the parking lot.

The bar phone rang. "Salty Dog."

"You okay there?" Max asked over the phone. "Did you close early?"

"I did, but it still came down faster than even I expected."

"Need me to come down and help?"

"Nah, got it covered. I'll stay here tonight."

Both Max and Cole had been trained to expect any variance and adjust their strategy to get ahead of a problem before it became one. After hanging up with Max, Cole looked up the latest weather advisory on his phone and hoped Valerie had made good time. He'd call her to check in once he knew for certain she would no longer be on the road.

In his office, Sub whined as if bombs were going off outside and Armageddon was imminent.

"Don't worry." Cole squatted to scratch behind his ears. "You're not dying. There's another piece of bacon in your future. This isn't the end."

He gave Sub a special treat out of his desk drawer, reserved for special occasions, and the dog went to it like it was his last meal.

Cole walked to the front to evaluate the weak ceiling spots and see how they were faring, when he saw Valerie at the entrance, knocking on the door.

She looked like she'd gone for a swim, her clothes drenched, while she held what was left of the umbrella.

Chapter Fifteen

Cole reached for his keys and opened the door, tugging her inside. "Get in here."

"My car won't start." She wiped her dripping hair and handed him the umbrella pieces. "So much for riding with the angels."

"Guess you'll be staying with a SEAL instead. We're no angels but we can still cover you."

"I *can't* stay. Can you drive me home? It's not that far."

Cole looked out the window and shook his head. While he had taken plenty of risks in his life, he *never* took stupid ones.

"You'll have to stay here tonight. It's too dangerous to drive right now."

"Too *dangerous*? Don't be ridiculous."

"We're near a huge body of water, in case you hadn't noticed. We're not in any real danger, but I don't know about this roof. And the weather advisory just ordered residents to stay off the roads other than emergencies."

"But Gram... I don't want to leave her alone all night. I can't believe this. It's just rain, for God's sake. Why does everyone..." Her eyes widened and she startled. "Oh my gosh, what's that sound?"

"It's the rain, kicking up. Sounds like bricks, doesn't it?"

She covered her ears. "Oh, Lord."

"Call your grandmother and see if anyone that's closer can stay with her tonight. If you want, I can call someone."

While Valerie got on the phone, he went to the office and found some towels. Sub followed him out, and seeing Valerie, almost lost his shit. His tail wagged, his tongue lolled out, and he licked her hand, then shamelessly rolled over on his back.

"You stud," Cole said.

Valerie smiled and bent to pet Sub while she spoke on the phone. "Don't worry. I won't drive in this rain. Well, I don't think you should be *grateful* the car wouldn't start. I could be home by now. No, it's not a *sign*. It means the car's battery died, that's all. Gram, please be careful, and I'll see you in the morning."

Cole handed her a towel. "You can't be comfortable in those clothes."

She attempted to dry herself off, wiping her face first. Then her cheeks. That amazing wild hair that seemed to be expanding like the universe.

"Newsflash. I'm not. But what can I do?"

He grinned.

"I'm not getting naked, Cole."

"I couldn't possibly be *that* lucky." He walked toward the office. "I have a change of clothes in here."

"*Your* clothes?" She followed him into the office. "What are we talking? Board shorts?"

"Exactly." He pulled out a desk drawer and came out with an old pair of board shorts and a worn dark blue tee that read: Navy.

She studied them. "I guess I can't be picky at this point."

"Not if you want to be dry."

"I wish you had a fireplace."

He cocked his head. "Would you install a fireplace in any establishment on the Gulf Coast? The *sun* is our fireplace."

"Guess not, but it would have been romantic." She shrugged. "Cozy."

"Sorry to disappoint."

My kingdom for a fireplace!

She gave him a smirk and gestured him outside the office. He moved in that direction, slowly, hoping a change of heart would be forthcoming, but wound up having the door shut in his face.

"Yep. I'm not that lucky," he said to the door. "Confirmed."

"I heard that!" Valerie said.

"Good," he muttered.

He checked the windows and saw they were still solid and not rattling out of their frames. Outside the wind howled and waves crashed. Lightning flashed like a laser show, and thunder struck three seconds later. Sub whined.

"Easy, boy." He bent to pat his head. "We'll get through this night. For once, it might be easier for you than me, but we'll get through this."

"Cole!" Valerie shouted from inside the office. "Big surprise. These shorts don't fit me."

"Wear the towel."

"That's funny."

"Or wear your wet clothes, but I should warn you. It's wet T-shirt contest time with that shirt."

She groaned. "Now you tell me."

"You know me. I'm not that noble. Am I, Sub?"

Sub whined and wagged his tail.

Valerie slowly opened the door. His T-shirt, at least, was long on her. The board shorts were perfect around that curvy and round very female ass that always had his full attention.

"I hope they don't tear." She tugged at the T-shirt, biting her lower lip.

"Well, at least they'd die happy."

"Stop teasing me," she said, but there was a little smile tugging at her lips.

"Never."

She ignored that and bent to pick up her wet clothes. "Um, I was thinking that I could spread my clothes out on the dishwasher rack?"

Valerie followed him into the kitchen with the industrial-size dishwasher. He opened it, and finding it had fortunately already been emptied, accepted her clothes and started to layer them. She slid him a look and handed him her bra and panties. They weren't boring cotton things but looked silky and soft. Frilly black lace thong and matching bra. Meaning she wasn't wearing either. Dear Lord, he was going to die. He should get an award at the entrance to heaven: Best Self Control around a Gorgeous Woman.

C'mon up and get your pin, Cole! Congratulations!

He shut the dishwasher door and faced her. "Do you have any other ways to torture me?"

"I'm not trying to torture you, baby," she said in a honeyed voice that sent heat curling through him.

"It just comes naturally?"

"I thought we decided."

"You decided." He crossed his arms and leaned against the dishwasher. "I went along."

"I mean, we've changed. Haven't we? I mean, I sure *hope* we have."

"I've grown up. That's what changed for me."

"But we both proved that we're no good at sustaining long-term relationships. Back then, we didn't know that. Now we do."

"Bullshit."

She blinked. "It's not."

He took her hand. "Did it ever occur to you that we were with the wrong people and that's why the relationships didn't last?"

"It did." She threaded her fingers through his. "I had such a hard time getting over you."

"In case you hadn't noticed, I'm invested. I can't go a day without thinking about you or talking to you." Cole met her eyes. "And there are schools here in Charming. You could stay, Valerie. Stay here with me."

She cocked her head and smiled up at him, as if he'd just said the last thing she'd ever expected to hear. "I mean, it's possible. Sure."

He brought her hand to his lips and kissed it.

She gave him a sweet smile, but he didn't miss that her lower lip trembled ever so slightly. "We were good together. Every *summer*. For the rest of the year? We don't know."

"Then we find out." He tugged her into his arms, gratified when she came quite willingly, offering no resistance.

"I'm not this person that everyone else sees. Sometimes I'm exhausted at the end of the day from putting on this act. Perky, flirty, happy. *Charming*. I'm independent, and I don't like asking for help."

"What? You could have fooled me," he deadpanned.

"I guess I'm like my grandmother that way. But I get in funks sometimes. I'm not always all that wonderful with people. Like, some of the parents of my students. Certain *men*. But my kids love me because I rarely have a bad day. In front of them."

"I know," Cole said, pressing his forehead to hers. "And I see exactly who you are. You're strong, and tough on the outside. A little creamy on the inside. You have a huge heart and I've always known that. No, you don't have your shit together all the time. None of us do. But with us, I like my odds."

"Just like that?"

In the end, it would be entirely up to him to talk her into staying. This time, she didn't have to go back at the end of the summer. He could keep her. It was up to him to figure out how.

"Entirely up to you. I'll be your willing love slave forever if you'll have me."

"Don't say that." She brought her fingertip to his lips.

"I am saying it. Until you walked into this bar, I didn't think I'd ever *feel* anything again. Not here." He moved her hand over his heart.

"Cole," she whispered. "I'm a hot mess."

"You're *not* a mess."

"Do you really want me in your life right now?"

"That depends. Are you staying?"

"I could."

"Then I don't know how I can make myself any clearer than this." He met her lips in a scorching hot kiss that yes, thank you, she returned.

The kiss grew hot and erotic in seconds as they reached for each other, tugging and pulling. He pushed her up against the industrial-size refrigerator, and hand under a knee, urged her to wrap her leg around him. She did, then reached behind and her hair tumbled around her shoulders, loose and free.

"You remember me." He'd loved nothing more than to grab on to a fistful of her wavy soft hair as he drove into her.

"I remember everything about you. Everything."

She kissed him again, not holding anything back. Deep, hot kisses, her warm hands under his shirt teasing and caressing.

Sub twisted around their legs, distracted from the storm by their actions. It was the one thing to pry Cole's attention away from this moment. This wasn't going to happen in his kitchen, against the cold refrigerator door.

He took Valerie's hand and led her to the office.

Valerie was about to do something stupid or… wonderful.

But she didn't want an audience, human or animal, to watch her and whatever crazy and impetuous thing she was about to do. Because this might be impulsive and senseless, totally outside of her wheelhouse, but this was a man she'd once trusted with her life. Surprisingly, that hadn't changed. Even if her judgment had been off about so many other things, she trusted him. If this was a mistake, they would make it together. They would hold hands while they jumped off a cliff. Just like before. But this time she had a deep sense that this wasn't wrong. She still loved him, right or wrong. Crazy or impulsive. Maybe she'd never stopped. The thought stilled her for a moment. How many people got a second chance like this?

So she would do this. Leave her old life behind and start over again. Terrifying. And liberating.

Cole reached inside a desk drawer and came out with a rawhide bone the size of a small boulder. Even Valerie caught the smell of bacon. Sub pranced around in a circle as if ready to perform tricks on demand. Then Cole executed a few hand signals. Sub lay on the floor and played dead for several seconds, until Cole gave him another hand signal.

"Wow. Impressive."

"I let him have this whenever I need him to be quiet because I have a meeting, an important phone call, or the health inspector is coming by. Special occasions." He gave the bone to Sub, who happily trotted to his bed in the corner. "He will now forget we exist."

Thunder struck again. Valerie startled and inched closer to Cole. Sub indeed seemed oblivious, proving bacon was his Achille's Heel.

Outside, the downpour continued. She heard it as

it smashed against the roof and windows, and furious winds whipped. She'd forgotten how the weather could change so quickly in the middle of the day in Texas. Maybe because she hadn't been back to Charming in the summer since after college graduation. Greg didn't like Texas and also didn't want Valerie to visit.

"You just want to see if you can hook up with that old boyfriend of yours. The summer-loving dude." Greg would tease her.

Because, yes, she'd told him about Cole. Naturally, she'd told Greg that they'd been far more casual than they actually had. A simple teenage crush that hadn't lasted. Burned itself out. She'd lied. But when she'd pictured seeing Cole again, when she pictured any type of reunion, it had never been like this. Not with this sweet hot intensity and ache that wouldn't subside. Or with this idea that they might pick up where they'd left off. That wasn't *possible*. They were different people than they'd been.

But maybe they could find out exactly *what* was possible. If anything at all.

Cole tugged her into his arms, kissing her hard and, as always, she forgot everything else around her. The sounds of the brick-like rain hitting the roof barely registered. Same for the thunder that boomed. Only Cole filled her thoughts. This man who saw her for the strong woman she'd always been, and wanted her anyway. Her hands drifted under his shirt and glided up and down his back, finally resting at the waistband of his board shorts, where she tugged.

She felt him smile against her lips and he tugged her hips against his so she could feel his erection. "Easy, girl."

"Why?" she whispered against his lips.

"We're going to have to improvise a little."

There were four walls in the office, but one had a closet door, the other shelves, a third the only window, and the fourth had several surfboards lined up against it. So much for sex against a wall, which she was more than certain Cole could pull off. She nearly laughed out loud at the thought that she'd been willing to have sex against a wall. Or a freezer door.

There was a love seat in the corner, but it didn't look big enough to fit Cole, who was at least six feet. She was in the middle of berating herself for an appalling lack of imagination when outside a loud boom echoed and the lights flickered, then went out.

Chapter Sixteen

Valerie should have anticipated this. No power. A horrible and empty feeling surged through her. "Cole!"

A warm hand settled on her low back. "I'm right here, baby."

In the pitch-black dark, she reached for him, any part of him. She wound up with something hard, and long.

His arm.

"I can't see you."

He flipped on a flashlight. "Surprised my generator hasn't kicked in yet. It better."

"Please. Don't let go of me."

"Never." He held her close, his hand gliding up and down her spine in a soothing motion.

The lights came back on in the next few seconds and Cole sighed. "I didn't even want to *think* about losing all that meat in the freezer."

She hadn't even considered that. Good for Cole, thinking on his feet, while she stood here, scared, but still finding the sparc time to drool over the hot surfer guy.

His dimples flashed, and he set the flashlight down, his gaze slowly traveling up her body. "How are we doing?"

"I don't know how *we're* doing, but as for me, I'm worried we're going to float away."

"Glad you didn't drive home?"

"What's going to happen to us?" She pressed her face against his chest.

"Nothing is going to happen to you. I've got you. I won't let anything happen to you."

"This is bad, right? This storm?"

"Nah, it's not bad until it's a hurricane. This is just a crazy Texas storm. We're going to live." His hand slid up and down her back. "Tomorrow there'll be some cleanup to do, but all the cars will still be where we left them. I guarantee you."

"Oh, good."

"Though I'm not sure about this roof." He glanced up at the ceiling.

She fisted his shirt. "Oh no. The roof. The repairs. The Historical Society."

"Don't worry about any of that."

"How can I not worry? I don't want you to lose this bar. That's it. I'm dropping out of the race."

"No, you are not." He traced the curve of her jaw.

She went quiet then, her arms around his waist, his powerful arms circling her. As usual, she was wasting valuable time worrying about things that may or may not happen. "Cole?"

"Yeah?"

"I'm about to tackle you to the ground."

"We can do better than that." He stepped away, then swiftly swept everything off his desk with one hand. "I hate paperwork."

She snorted and glanced at the papers, pens and one book on the ground. It seemed to be about nautical weather patterns. "Anything important there?"

"Nothing at all."

He walked her to his desk where he easily lifted and sat her on the edge. Smiling, he traced the curve of her jaw with his thumb, then her lips. He followed that same path with his lips and tongue. His kiss was its usual blend of blazing hot with tender trails that found their way to her heart. She lost her tight control. Her hands were under his shirt, gliding up and down his spine, reveling in his warm, taut skin. He stopped kissing her long enough to pull off his shirt one-handed in a move so exquisitely male that she nearly came on the spot.

The tattoo that she'd noticed on his bicep actually wound around his shoulder and back.

She pulled off her shirt. Nothing but bare skin

here, no helpful sexy presentation from her black push-up bra. Just 100 percent her. Naked. Given his heated gaze, he didn't miss the lingerie. She stood, tugging at the board shorts…*his* shorts, which were so tight around her hips she half worried she couldn't get them off now.

But like he wanted to be the one to have his hands between the cotton material and her naked behind, Cole gently tugged on the shorts, and as if they, too, loved his touch, they slid off her. Slowly. Good, maybe all they needed was their owner's hands. She didn't feel big or fleshy with Cole. She happened to be the right size for him, even if she frequently had to remind herself of that fact. But Cole had always made her feel like this. Beautiful in her own skin. Wanted. In that moment she realized she hadn't felt desired in far too long. She'd forgotten the sensation.

His lips lowered to her nipples, sucking, teasing and licking. Before long he'd whipped her into a frenzy. Shameless, she bucked against him, grabbing his steely butt, and pulling him between her suddenly wide-open legs.

"Do you…have something?"

Please let him have protection, because she didn't. And she couldn't stop now. She'd die. By the blank expression on his face, she could see his thoughts had run along the same lines. But then he searched rather enthusiastically through his desk drawer, pulled out his wallet and drew out a condom. He studied it.

"What are you doing?"

"Checking the expiration date." He ripped it open with his teeth. "We're good."

She nearly threw back her head in relief. He pulled down his board shorts and underwear, and she helped roll the condom on, stroking him until he groaned. Standing, he pulled her hips to the edge.

"Wrap your legs around me."

She did, and he entered in one long thrust that made her gasp. When he stopped moving, she egged him on by bucking against him.

"Don't stop," she moaned. "Please, Cole."

Like he'd been waiting for this moment, the control slipped from his handsome face, and he pumped into her. He buried himself inside of her and each stroke went deeper and harder. The pressure built deliciously. His thrusts were so powerful that the desk actually moved, and he met her eyes and smiled.

"Valerie," he said. "I missed this. You and me, we're so good together."

For two years, Valerie had shut down sexually. There had been no interest in anyone, and all it took was a man asking whether or not she wanted dessert on a date for her to assume it to be a comment about the seven additional pounds she'd gained after her divorce. Yes, she'd been overly sensitive, miserable and happy to be left alone at the end of a dinner date so she could curl up with a good book. Because fantasy kicked reality's ass.

Now, she almost didn't recognize the wanton woman she'd become. This woman had abandoned all inhibitions and knew exactly what she wanted. This woman was not a bit ashamed of her body, but proud of the pleasure it gave Cole. And somehow, she'd started to trust in her own judgment again, a little at a time. Probably because her trust odometer had never been off where it came to Cole. He'd always been real to her. So open, honest and rooted. Down-to-earth.

Cole reached between them to touch the tender, swollen spot at the base of all that heat and sensation at the same time as he nipped her neck. She came completely undone. Like every lace had been untied, and everything inside her unbuckled, she moaned, and shook, and trembled with an intense and wicked pleasure. He continued to drive into her, and a moment later he also shook and trembled as he came to his own release.

"I...can't...move," she said, lying splayed on the desk.

He pressed kisses following a path from her ankle, to the inside of her thighs, and her belly button, where he licked and teased at her silver ring. "I like this. It suits you."

The ring she wore now was one in the shape of a heart. She hadn't worn a navel ring for a while, but she'd had it pierced on the night she'd graduated from college with honors. Another friend had gotten a tattoo. It had seemed a time to celebrate new beginnings. And that night, she'd thought of Cole. She'd wondered if he'd get a piercing, or maybe a tattoo, since it seemed that all military guys did.

"Did you ever think about me?" she whispered.

It was a dangerous question to ask because Cole would not lie to her. But if he hadn't thought of her much, he'd still spare her feelings. He'd say something like, "Now and then," or "Sometimes."

This would mean "not really."

"All the time," he said and kissed her deeply.

And funnily enough, she believed him.

Afterward, they lay on the love seat, on every towel Cole probably owned. Her cheek pressed against Cole's chest, she listened to the steady thrum of his heart.

"You sure got a lot better at this," she said.

"I hope so," Cole said, kissing her temple. "Gotta say, this is one area in which I don't mind your fierce motivation to one-up me."

She laughed, because she didn't mind, either.

"I thought we would never be as good as I remembered, because that memory was so special, locked tight inside my heart. I didn't think reality would ever measure up to my memories of us."

"That makes sense. We all idealize our past." Our first love.

"Right, and that's exactly what I did. Everything I remembered about us was perfect. Frozen in time. We never fought, we never—"

You never cheated on me.

"Wait. What do you mean? We fought."

"I don't mean that last time."

"We argued. I can't believe you forgot."

She plopped her chin on his chest. "About what?"

"You were always hell on wheels and that's what I loved about you."

The words sliced through her with a sweetness she hadn't expected. She'd been in love for the first time in her life, arguably the only time, and expectations and plans were high in her teenage hormonal brain.

"But again, what did we actually argue about?"

After all, they hadn't argued finances or how they'd pay the rent that month. They hadn't hated each other's friends. They had the same friends. Didn't argue about family as she loved Angela, and Angela loved her. Gram loved Cole and Cole loved her. Then again, they'd never spent Thanksgiving together, or any other holiday that brought out the worst in family togetherness.

As if his thoughts echoed her own, he threaded his fingers through hers. "You're right. It was stupid stuff. We never fought."

"We're in the real world and that's going to change."

"Of course. We already have, over Mr. Charming."

She sat up straight. "We can't let anyone know about this. About us."

His hand, which had been caressing her back, suddenly froze. "Why not?"

She pressed her palm to his cheek. "I don't know, wouldn't that be best?"

"I don't think it matters."

"You're right. This fall, I'll be teaching somewhere in the district. This job is just temporary."

"But us." He rolled them, bracing himself above her. "We're not temporary. Not anymore."

"No," she said, her voice more breath than whisper.

Then Cole made love to her again, while outside the wind howled.

Chapter Seventeen

Valerie woke the next morning to a strange sound: silence.

The storm had passed.

Then Cole moved, and she recognized a couple of things in a hurry. It was morning, and she was splayed on top of something hard, warm, male. Her limbs were entangled with his, her lips and nose smushed against his neck.

She would stay. She'd started over once before after the divorce. This time, she'd do it not because she'd been forced to, but by choice.

"I could get used to this," Cole said groggily.

She smiled against his neck, feeling a sharp and

delicious warmth pulse through her. "Even if your legs dangled off this short couch all night?"

"Yep," he said, and then rose, lifting them both. "I'll make coffee."

"Hmm. I was so right about you. You're a prince."

"Or, you know, Mr. Charming." He winked.

Thoroughly enjoying the view, she lazily watched as his agile, naked body moved swiftly with utter male grace. He shoved on underwear, board shorts and a T-shirt.

Sub lazily lifted his sleeping head from his dog bed and stretched.

"Good morning, Sub." Valerie gave him a little finger wave.

He wagged his tail.

"Get my clothes, please?" she asked Cole.

"Way ahead of you." He left the office, Sub following closely behind.

Valerie climbed out of bed and went cautiously to the window, separating less than an inch of slat from the blinds and peeking through. The window faced part of the parking lot and she saw puddles here and there, but they were beginning to recede. The sun shone brightly, showering the beach with glistening rays.

"Good news. We hung on to our roof. How does it look outside?" Behind her, Cole stroked her naked back, his large palm coming to rest on her rump.

She leaned into him, wishing she could spend the

entire morning with him in this office, away from the rest of the world.

"Not bad."

He kissed her bare shoulder and handed her the now-dry clothes.

She turned in the circle of his arms, smiling into his beautiful blues. "Thank you."

"Do you have to go right away?"

"Why? What did you have in mind?"

He grinned. "A shower. At my place. You're going to love the wand's pulse setting."

"I won't need the shower pulse setting." She kissed him, slowly and leisurely. Deeply, while her fingers threaded through his silky hair. "But I do have to get home."

She had a phone call to make and she'd rather not do it in front of Cole.

"Gotta say, I love the way you tell me no."

"It's only no for now." She broke free of his embrace, which was admittedly difficult to do, and dressed quickly before he changed her mind.

She was somewhat hindered by the fact that he gave her a slow smile, arms crossed, and watched her get dressed as he leaned on the edge of his desk. Just the hot memory of the way they'd creatively used that surface last night had her heart, and other parts, throbbing.

"You keep doing that."

"What?"

"Trying to talk me out of leaving."

He held up both palms. "I haven't said another word."

"You don't have to. It's in that smile of yours that would talk the panties off a nun."

He winced. "Just want to talk your panties off."

"I just got them back on," she laughed. "Is that coffee ready?"

A few minutes later, she and Cole were both on their way back to Gram's mobile home park in his truck, Sub panting in the back seat. The minute they'd stepped out of the bar, Valerie breathed in the cooler temperatures that the storm left behind. It was nice enough outside that Cole rolled down the back windows for Sub, who had his head hanging out, enjoying the sights and smells.

"After I drop you off, I'll go back to see about your angel wagon. Hopefully it just needs a jump-start."

"Thank you for the ride," she said when he stopped in front of Gram's home.

He reached for her, pulling her close. "I'll call you later."

"Okay." She leaned into him again, that rock-solid presence that never failed to offer comfort.

They kissed and Valerie rushed inside the trailer, skipping over puddles.

"There you are!" Gram said from her recliner. "Lois left a few minutes ago and guess what! PT is canceled today. Hallelujah! The therapist had flooding at her place. I mean, I'm sorry about the flooding, but I could use a break from her sadism. And how did everything make out over at the boardwalk?"

"The Salty Dog made out fine as far as I could tell." She set her tote bag on the couch. "Cole was prepared as always."

"Have you eaten?"

"Just coffee. I'll make us some breakfast. First, I need to take a quick shower. My clothes feel damp and clammy on me."

"Go ahead. I'm watching *Family Feud*."

Oh, would that Valerie could be happy just checking out of life and watching *Family Feud* all day between meals. Or staying in bed with Cole all day. But she had problems to solve. People to call. After she'd phoned him, her father still hadn't called her back to suggest a proposed plan of action. She'd made it abundantly clear that they were on borrowed time.

He picked up almost immediately. "Hello, honey."

"Hey, I still haven't heard back from you, so I thought I'd call." She heard a loudspeaker in the background and wondered if he was out shopping.

"Don't worry. She's my mother and I'm *going* to take care of her."

"Yes, but I told you exactly how to do that. We'll have to be careful about this, so that she doesn't find out I called you."

But she'd done so in the end. For one thing, she wanted Cole to have the Mr. Charming money to fix his bar. If she won, she'd already decided that she wanted to give it to him and Max. Secondly, she was no longer certain the money would come in time. Gram didn't have to know *how* Valerie solved this problem. Gram hadn't realized how much her husband had taken care of her when he was alive. She wouldn't have to know how Valerie had managed, either. Even though Valerie was determined to educate Gram, now was *not* the time. Now had to be the time for action. Later, financial education.

"And I heard you, but I have to do things my way."

"What *way*? Did you deposit the money in her account yet? Are you going to wire it to me?"

And then she heard the loudspeaker again. The distinctive sound of a ticket agent over the airport's intercom.

…*Gate 23, boarding now.*

Dread spiked through her, but maybe…yes, sure, maybe her father was taking a trip. To a…work conference. Of course, that had to be it. Because he *knew,* Valerie had distinctly told him, that Gram was still not over the divorce. That she didn't want his help.

"Dad, where are you?"

"I'm at the St. Louis Airport. I should arrive in Austin late this afternoon. Then I'll drive down. I have a short layover in Dallas. It's not a good flight but the best I could on such short notice."

Valerie clutched the phone. "*Excuse* me?"

"I figure, depending on traffic, I'll be in Charming this evening."

"Apparently you heard nothing I told you!"

"I heard it all. This has gone on long enough."

"You don't get to decide how long this goes on. She's your mother, and you need to respect her wishes."

"And you're my daughter. Whatever happened to respecting *my* wishes? I made a mistake, and I've paid for it long enough. What about forgiveness?"

Oh my gosh, it was just like a cheater to beg for forgiveness. Greg had done the same. "You can ask for forgiveness from Mom, and maybe even from me, but you can't ask it from Gram."

"Exactly, because I didn't *do* anything to my mother, except offend her religious sensibilities."

"It's about more than that and you know it." Valerie took a breath. "How am I supposed to explain this to her? I went directly against her wishes and now she's going to be angry with me, too. What have you done? I should have *never* trusted you."

"Take a deep breath and calm down. I've got a plan and she doesn't need to know you called me for help."

"I won't lie to Gram. I can't."

"You won't have to. Let me do that."

Valerie snorted. She couldn't help that. "Of course. You're so good at it."

"I'll see you soon."

Valerie understood her father's perspective but walking into this situation the way he planned was not the smartest move. While Valerie figured how to manage the hurricane named Rob Villanueva headed her way, she had one more phone call to make. There was no longer any doubt in her mind that after last night, she was staying. She had a second chance with Cole and she couldn't just walk away from that.

She dialed Ann Marie Carroll, the principal of her school. Valerie had signed her teaching contract at the end of April. Though there was never a lack of teachers in their district, giving a month's notice was the least she could do for her mentor and colleague.

"You've caught me at a good time," Ann Marie said. "The kids are at summer camp and I've got the morning all to myself."

The last time she'd seen Ann Marie, they'd been discussing the plans they had to raise funds for a new library. Valerie cleared her throat. "I don't know how to say this, so I'm just going to say it."

"Oh, no. Don't say it. You and Greg are back together?"

"Lord, no!"

"Thank goodness. After what he did to you, I'm honestly surprised you still talk to him. Or her."

It had almost been a small-town scandal. *Teacher's husband cheats with her colleague.* And it had definitely been a scandal in their little community. Valerie had refused to leave the school where they both taught, and so Regina had left.

"I have to. We still own a house together."

"He still hasn't sold it?" she screeched. "I thought that was in the divorce .settlement."

"It is and if I take him back to court, it will be enforced."

"Oh, Valerie." Ann Marie sighed.

"But that's not why I'm calling." Valerie cleared her throat. "I'm not returning to school this fall. I'm sorry."

"Honey, don't let them do this to you! You have the right to live and work in this community, too. I thought we were past all this."

"That's not why. I'm staying because I want to. No other reason. I…love it here. I always have, I just never pictured…"

That Cole and I would have a second chance.

There was a beat of silence. "Is your grandmother doing any better?"

"Oh, she definitely is. She's using a walker and will probably be back to her old self soon."

"Well, I'm disappointed, but I understand. I lose at least one teacher every summer. Usually when a husband transfers out of state."

"I'm sorry. This wasn't my intention. When I signed the contract, I meant to come back."

"At least you will leave this scandal in your rear-view. Greg and Regina will be history and you'll never have to see either one of them again." She passed. "But damn, I'll miss you."

"Me, too." It seemed Valerie had something in her eye now as it filled with tears. "But I'll visit."

Her roommate would send Valerie's things, and

she'd eventually be forced to return at least once to enforce the settlement.

It just wouldn't be anytime soon.

After Cole headed home to take a shower and change, he took Sub for a long walk along the stretch of the beach next to the lighthouse. With a garbage bag, he picked up anything that had drifted onto the shore and didn't belong. He only had to do this after a big storm like this one, but there was no end to what he might find on the beach. Plastic bags and food wrappers were common, but he'd once found a baby's pacifier. A condom. The reason he never failed to wear gloves. He considered this stretch of the beach his private sanctuary. Not the best surfing spot in town, but today that would be debatable.

Waves crested higher than normal, making him want to bring out his board, but he had to get back to the bar. Though he hadn't wanted to share yet with Valerie, the roof was leaking. Cole had set up some buckets before he'd left and phoned Max. They'd assess their situation today and come to a decision. They might have to close down and just the thought of putting his staff on furlough pissed him off.

Cole passed shops opening up, business as usual. Max was already inside. Unfortunately, so was Ralph Mason, carrying a clipboard and wearing a hard hat.

"They're closing us down," Max said.

Cole barely held back a curse. "For how long?"

"As long as it takes," Ralph said.

"Ballpark?" Max pressed.

Ralph glanced at the roof. "A month?"

"Do what you have to do," Cole said, truly disgusted, as he walked back to the office.

A few minutes later, Max joined Cole and together they began to make calls to the staff, giving them the ugly news. Closed for an undetermined period of time. He'd tell Valerie in person this afternoon.

"I wish my old man was here right now, forced to make these calls instead of us," Cole said from behind his desk.

But he hadn't seen Lloyd since he'd gone over to have a talk with him. He'd done a good job of staying away from the bar, and Cole had been too busy to check in. Besides, he'd meant it. Something had to change. Cole refused to indulge him any longer. It was one thing to be kind, and another to be an enabler. No more. He'd never threatened calling the cops on Lloyd before, and he must have understood Cole meant it.

"I'm looking into cashing out part of my IRA," Max said, feet propped on Cole's desk.

Though Max was good with money, he lived modestly, and he had money—much of it tied up in long-term investments.

"I can't let you do that."

"Not your decision," Max said. "I like Charming. This place has grown on me."

"It does have a way of doing that."

Cole pulled out the flask he kept in a drawer of his

desk. He took a pull and handed it to Max. They used to drink more often than they did now, and funny how owning a bar had changed all that.

"I ran into Ava earlier and she said so far the initial results show you far in the lead."

"Yeah, well, it's not over until it's over."

"You *do* want to win this, don't you?" Max narrowed his eyes.

"And I will."

When it came time to call Valerie, Cole took his phone and stepped outside. Waves crashed and the beach was deserted.

She answered on the first ring. "Hi."

"Got some bad news, baby. They've closed us down. You're out of a job for now. We all are."

"I thought everything was okay. Was there much damage?"

"The roof was weak in places and it didn't do well with that amount of pressure. The Historical Society has closed us down until we get the repairs done."

"How long will that be?"

He heard the worry and concern in her voice, and it slayed him. "A month, maybe?"

"Oh, Cole. What can I do? How can I help?"

"We've got it under control. I'm just sorry your temporary job has turned out to be far more temporary than either of us had planned."

"It's okay." She paused for a beat. "I think my situation…it's going to be fixed soon."

"The reason you needed the money."

"Yes. It was for my grandmother. She was going to lose her home, and I couldn't let that happen."

He froze, his stomach pitched, and he cursed. "You should have told me that!"

"Why? So you could feel sorry for me and drop out of the contest?" She paused. "I have a little pride too, you know?"

"A *little*? I would have felt like a chump if I'd won and your grandmother lost her house."

"That wouldn't have happened because I would have found another way. And she wouldn't let me tell anyone, if you must know. I honored her wishes as long as I could."

He snorted. "Baby, you're too competitive."

"Too competitive? Look who's talking." She laughed softly. "We're quite a pair."

He shook his head, chuckling.

He'd never noticed how much she was like him.

Chapter Eighteen

Once again, Valerie had no job. But she would be okay. Summers were usually her time off and she had a little savings put away to get her through the summer. Not enough to help Gram, unfortunately. But she felt much worse for Salty Dog employees like Debbie, a single mom with three children. There had to be a way. A work-around. Surely they didn't have to close down the bar entirely?

Once Valerie cleaned the house, made lunch and binge watched reruns of *Gilmore Girls* with Gram, she could no longer avoid the subject.

"What would you like for dinner?" Valerie asked. "Because it looks like we'll be having company."

"Oh? Will Cole be joining us?" Gram winked.

"No...and out of curiosity, why would you say that?"

"Just something Lois said the other night. And that photo of you two? Honey, he has it bad for you."

"Really? Why? What did Lois say?" She was about as interested as a sixth grader with her first real crush.

"That Cole couldn't take his eyes off you."

Despite everything else on her mind, Valerie couldn't help the warm sensation that rippled through her. "Well... I've decided to move here."

Gram clapped her hands. "Thank the good Lord! It will be so good to have you close. Finally, you will give *someone* else a chance."

"But I still have to settle everything back home. I need to find a teaching position here. I'll be starting all over."

"Don't think of it as starting over. Think of it as a new beginning."

"That's the same thing." Still she loved Gram's attitude of seeing the better side of a problem.

It *would* be a new beginning.

"Gram, the person joining us for dinner. It's... your son." Valerie refused to lie to her grandmother even by omission. "Before you say anything..."

But Gram held out her palm like a stop sign. "Why is he coming? Why now?"

"He may have heard from me that you need some help."

"Why would you do that, *mija*? I asked you not to. Your grandfather and I never asked anyone for help."

"Because you're too proud, but I'm sure Papa would have been fine with asking your only son for help."

"No, I don't believe that. He'd be humiliated to need his son's help."

"Is that what you think? That *you* should feel humiliated? Because there's no need for that. Papa didn't educate you on your finances the way he should have."

She shook a finger. "Don't say anything bad about your Papa. He always took care of me. Of us."

Valerie sighed. "I know he did, but he should have explained a few things to you."

"He paid off our home, and insurance for a year in advance. What more could he have done?"

"You could have been his partner if he'd allowed you to be. Sometimes letting a man simply take care of you, and not bother with the details, isn't such a good thing."

"We're going to be just fine. I made a vision board."

"A *vision* board?"

"It's this new thing they're doing at the senior center during craft time. Lois has been a couple of times now and she told me all about it. Lois and I created our vision boards. We're manifesting. I cut out photos of money. A photo of a cute little house in Charming for you, and a nice new car. Lois had cut out photos of couples, weddings and hearts. Not two days after she made her board, Roy suggested they go together to your kickoff event! And now, you're going to move here. This works, honey! The money is coming, too."

Valerie face-palmed. "How?"

Because she had a pretty good idea of when, and by her calculations it could be in another few minutes, give or take traffic from Austin.

"We don't know how or when. You'll see. Have a little faith."

Valerie had never been one to put her life in the hands of pure faith. She had a plan. Always.

"You've got to stop being so stubborn. Please, let's just talk to him and see what he has to say."

"It had better be an apology."

If her father was wise, he'd start there. But unfortunately, like mother like son with those two. If he hadn't apologized after his father's death, or his mother's stroke, why would he now?

"Where does he plan on staying?" Gram said.

"Probably the inn."

"He's always been so *wasteful* with money." She clucked. "He shouldn't be just flying out to Texas for no good reason. Your Papa would not approve."

"Let's just be civil, okay? Hear him out." Valerie would try full-on begging next.

Gram settled back in her recliner chair and crossed her arms, lips pursed. "Fine, but don't go anywhere."

Not when she'd be required to referee. She'd

hoped to see Cole tonight, if even for a short time, but that probably wouldn't happen now.

Only thirty minutes later, a rental car pulled up outside. Dad unloaded a suitcase and a bag from the trunk. She hadn't seen him in a while, because she'd never liked Savannah, his second wife, and the feeling had been mutual. He looked almost resigned, his tall figure slumped, no longer the handsome man that had once turned heads. A professor and Antonio Banderas look-alike, he'd had his fair share of students after him, Savannah just one of many.

Valerie met him at the door. "I told her you were coming because I'd asked for your help."

"Good."

"She's not thrilled, just so you know."

"Big surprise there."

Her gaze dropped to his luggage. "Um, I see you have a couple of bags with you. Where are you staying?"

He looked at her like she'd asked him for directions to the moon. "Here, where else?"

"This is a two-bedroom house."

"I'll take the couch. Are you going to let me inside?"

Valerie moved aside as she'd been blocking the door. "I was about to start dinner."

Dad stepped inside, which meant he was already in the great room as there was no foyer in the small home. The easy chairs faced the TV, which meant Gram's back was to her son. She seemed to be doing her best to ignore he was on the same planet, let alone in the same room.

"Look who's here," Valerie said, employing some of her third grade teacher skills. "Isn't this nice?"

"Marni." Dad set his bags near the couch and took a seat. "How are you?"

"Hmph," Gram said. "Depends on the day."

"How about today?"

"*Not* good."

"Okay," Valerie said in her singsong voice. "I'm going to make dinner."

Greg used to call this her "idiot" voice. As in, *Don't talk to me like I'm an idiot.* She never did, since her third graders weren't, as Greg so kindly referred to them, "idiots." But *some* people behaved like children, and when they did, Valerie never failed to treat them as such.

As she chopped tomatoes and onions for the spaghetti sauce, she listened to faint talking barely distinguishable over the TV. The deep but stern sounds of her father's voice: *doing the best I can, want to help, you should have called me...*

But not a single "I'm sorry I disappointed you."

They ate pasta at the table while mostly staring at each other in between bites. Occasionally Dad would ask about the weather. Valerie studied her father, hoping he'd just pay up and take the next plane ride home. Dad looked to Gram, seeming to silently implore her to hear him out. Gram looked from Valerie to Dad, lip curled in disapproval.

After dinner, they headed back to the great room, Dad reaching out to guide Gram's walker, her continuing to slap his hand away.

"Valerie, could I have a moment to speak to your grandmother in private?" he asked.

"She's not going anywhere," Gram protested.

"Mami, this is between you and me. You've brought Valerie into a matter that should have been between mother and son."

"She didn't—" Valerie began.

He held up his palm. "Regardless. I know you wanted to help and it's in your nature. But let me talk with my mother for a few minutes, would you? Why not just go for a little drive? It's a nice night."

"She doesn't have a car," Gram said.

"What happened to the car?" Dad boomed.

"It wouldn't start in the storm. Probably the battery."

"I'll take a look at it tomorrow."

"Sure. Thanks."

Dad had no idea what he was doing under the hood, so if it wasn't a dead battery he would be of no help. But Mom believed this was the one area in which her dad felt he could be of any help at all to Valerie, and that for some reason, men were forever trying to fix things.

She grabbed the umbrella she'd taken from the car as she would never be caught without one again. "I think I'll take a walk instead."

She'd stroll a little on this beautifully warm night.

Outside, the air was clear and crisp, the sunset a glorious splash of red and pink hues. She wondered what the sunset looked like from the lighthouse. Seagulls could be heard squawking in the distance, and waves crashed. Pulling out her camera phone, she took a few shots. She played with the filter app she'd installed on her phone, amazed at how far some apps had come.

She took a few more pictures and admired the aperture. She hadn't walked long before she used the phone for its main function, and dialed Cole.

He answered on the first ring. "Hey, baby. You okay?"

"I'm good."

"Took your grandma's wagon to the shop. Turns out it needs a new battery. I'll get it to you soon."

She gave a little gratified smile at the sound of his voice. After Greg and Regina, Valerie's self-confidence had taken a serious hit. She'd only been on three first dates since the divorce. Always fixed up by well-meaning friends, always ending in "meh" feelings all around and zero follow-up. Her girlfriends seemed to think she'd be drawn to the accountant, engineer, lawyer…straitlaced types.

Been there, done that.

Not once had she been fixed up with a charismatic bartender, mechanic, or a hot former navy SEAL. Then again, those were probably few and far between. She'd sort of hit the jackpot with Cole Kinsella. Anyone would. But he was *hers* now, again, and the thought wanted to bubble up inside until it spilled over like champagne bubbles. Her heart pulsed in a sweet rhythm. Dangerous stuff.

"What's up?" Cole said.

"Just going for a walk and I have an idea of how we might rescue the Salty Dog."

"Wish you wouldn't worry about this."

"How can I not worry? Debbie's a single mom and I'm pretty sure everyone who works there can't afford a month off on furlough. And really, when's the last time you heard of a renovation coming in on time and on budget?"

He let out a small groan. "Okay, let me have your idea."

"Don't worry about a thing. I'll take care of it."

Valerie continued to walk down the empty, narrow streets of the senior citizen park. Pride of ownership existed in this neighborhood. Little balconies were filled with colorful, boxed flowers. The tree-lined streets were lit with solar fairy lights. This happened every evening in Charming, straight through Christmas, she'd heard.

"Cole, you should know I'm dropping out of the contest."

"We discussed this. Don't."

"Why not? I want you and Max to have the money."

"Maybe I want you to have the money."

"That's sweet, but—"

"Don't worry. Max and I are on it. We have a plan. And Max says that just the publicity of my entering

Mr. Charming, not to mention the event, has helped. Thanks to you."

"Thanks to me?"

"The whole theme was your idea and you put it all together. If it had been up to me, I would have just put up a sign that said Event, and asked people to show up."

"You're more creative than that." She hushed her voice. "You proved it last night."

He chuckled, a deep scraping sound that gave her an all-body tingle. "Point taken. But I was motivated."

For a moment, they were both so quiet she could hear the sound of her own heartbeat.

"We both were."

Changing the subject before they both got too worked up, Valerie went on to safer topics. "It's not fair to thank me for the event because it helped me, too. I did it for me, and also for you, because you're my...my Cole."

"I'm your Cole."

"You know what I mean."

"Just teasing you. But I don't want you to drop out. I mean it."

"You're so sweet to me."

"Because I need to beat you fair and square."

"Hey!"

She nearly laughed at that true statement. Good to know he wasn't going to let her take it easy based on their recent relationship shift. Just in case she'd forgotten how competitive they'd both been.

"I thought I'd softened you up."

"I believe I'm the one who softened *you* up."

"I don't think so. I softened you. It was clear."

"There was literally nothing soft about me last night. But let's just say there was a little bit of softening on your end. Quite a little. As in *a lot*."

She thought she might add to his comments about last night, but she'd already started to get a little hot just thinking about it. Whew!

"Well, you…okay, we can do this all night long."

"Now *that* sounds promising. I'm in. Let's do it all night."

"I know I can, not sure about you."

He waited only a beat. "Challenge accepted."

"Listen, I better hang up before I wind up running all the way to the lighthouse."

His chuckle was low and deep. "Just in case, I'll leave the door unlocked. Maybe even wide open. I do have Sub, after all. I'll be the one upstairs without any clothes on."

She managed to hang up, somehow, even if there was another short discussion about which one of them was more confident they could handle themselves in case of a break-in brought about by him leaving the door unlocked.

It seemed that their competition had become friendly, as Ava had assumed from the beginning. At the time, it hadn't been. But now Valerie was flushed with affection for Cole. His slow easy smile, eyes glittering with intelligence. His arms wrapped around her. Her hands gliding down his strong forearms and under his shirt.

Contrary to what Greg believed, she hadn't come to Charming for Cole. But unexpectedly, every possibility under the black velvet sky had opened up.

Even ones she'd have never imagined.

Chapter Nineteen

When Valerie got back to the house, Gram had retired to bed earlier than normal, and Dad sat on the couch watching the sports channel. He shut the TV off the moment Valerie closed the door.

"I'll need to see all the finances tomorrow morning."

"What did Gram say?"

"The usual. I let her down, my father, you, your mother, God, country and... I may have forgotten someone else."

"What did she tell you about her *situation*?"

"Nothing, of course. Other than I shouldn't worry because Papa would have hated to ask for my help. She seems to think the money will materialize out of thin air. And she obviously has no idea that bank institutions are not our friends."

"That was Papa's fault. He took care of her. A little too well."

"Not much we can do about that now. My father was old school."

Valerie plopped down next to him. "Dad, what are you really doing here?"

"What do you mean? I'm here because you called."

"I didn't ask you to fly here. How can you just pick up and leave like this? What about Savannah?"

Dad's second wife was far younger than him and fairly controlling. Gram not being her biggest fan had long been an issue between all three of them. The last time any of them had seen Savannah had been Papa's funeral nearly two years ago, and even that had been a tense few hours. Savannah had done her duty, then hopped on a plan back to Missouri.

"We haven't been getting along."

"Oh boy. What did you do?"

He scowled. "Why do you assume I did something wrong?"

"Um, the best predictor of future behavior..."

"I was a happily married man for sixteen years. Then, I made one mistake. One. I couldn't have possibly learned my lesson?"

"Well..."

He lowered his head. "She left me."

Valerie wasn't shocked. Every time she'd seen them together the tension had been thick, and not the good kind of tension. Savannah was nearly twenty years younger than Dad. But no matter what her father had done, Valerie saw only a middle-aged man who'd just been clobbered by the karma stick.

"I'm sorry."

"You're not. I deserve this, don't I? Your mother was perfect for me, but I got my head turned around by a younger woman. That makes me the biggest cliché in the world. I don't know whether Mami will be happy about this breakup, or whether this is just another disappointment."

"I'm not sure, either. But I'll bet there are some I-told-you-sos thrown in there."

"No doubt." He dragged a hand through his slightly receding hairline. "You never did tell me what happened between you and Greg. And I suppose you're not going to tell me now."

"He cheated on me. With one of my friends."

He cursed under his breath. "I'm sorry, honey."

"Honestly, somewhere along the way I fell out of love with him. Maybe it was wrong, but I had to try and make my marriage work. I didn't want to fail, so I stuck it out, even though I was miserable. No wonder he found someone else."

He cursed again, this time in Spanish. Valerie wanted to remind her father that he was hardly in the position to judge Greg. But there might be an honor code among cheaters, like the one among thieves.

Thou shall not cheat with thy wife's friends.

"Dad, you never told me what happened between you and Mom."

He blinked. "You *know* what happened."

"I know her side of the story."

"You want to hear my side? I thought I didn't get to have a side."

She squirmed. "Maybe now I want to know a cheating husband's side of things."

"Why?"

"Because of Greg. I never want to make that mistake again."

Her eyes were misting, damn it, but now the pain was in the humiliation of having been disrespected. The embarrassment of being the proverbial last to know. She'd tried so hard not to be one of them. A woman who didn't see what should have been obvious.

Anytime Greg was out of town for business, coincidentally Regina had been, too.

Dad placed a solid hand on hers. "Don't you dare blame yourself. There is no reason good enough for a man to cheat on his wife."

"Then why?"

"Because some men are weak and immature. Your mother was good to me, but she…she just didn't need me anymore. Maybe because we'd been married so long, I felt invisible. I know, I should have told her, we could have worked it out. Gone to counseling. But I've since learned that I'm not big on talking about my feelings. Also, the feelings seemed ridiculous even to me, so voicing them out loud to my wife? I couldn't do that. But they didn't go away. I wanted to be needed. To be seen. And then Savannah came along and acted like I was a superhero. It was addicting."

Valerie considered how incredibly needy and codependent Regina had been. It was the single least attractive quality about her for Valerie, but obviously not to a man who wasn't getting along with his wife. Valerie hadn't *ever* needed Greg. She'd been proud to be on her own, to be independent, and he'd just slid into her life.

She'd always thought it a good thing to be self-sustaining. While being independent was a good thing, maybe she could have done with a little less pride.

And maybe sometimes, it wasn't always such a terrible thing to need someone.

The next morning, Gram and Dad were sitting at the kitchen table, Dad's laptop between them. Gram had worked her voice into a whine she only used for the physical therapist.

"But I don't understand the spreadsheets!"

"That's why I'm trying to explain, if you'd just listen."

"Dad, maybe start with something a little less techy?" Valerie said. "Like the checkbook register, perhaps?"

His eyes widened. "Does she still have one?"

She pointed to the folder with all the financial statements and paperwork she'd accumulated. "Yes."

"Well, the first thing we'll do is get you moved to online banking. You wouldn't believe how easy it is. You press a button, and bam! A bill is paid. On time, without a stamp."

"I don't trust that," Gram said. "Those people will hack me and take all my money."

"They can't *do* that. Or the Federal Trade Commission will be after them."

"Hmph," Gram said, shaking her head. "And if I push the wrong button? What about that, genius?"

When Valerie left, she had no doubt where she'd gotten her stubborn gene.

Last night, Dad had offered use of his car rental until he "had a chance to look at the car." Valerie took him up on his offer because she had work to do, and quickly. Her first stop was to a lovely coffee shop she'd seen in town. They had several large parasol umbrellas lining the storefront, but in this oppressive heat, they were rarely occupied. Only, at the mention of Cole and "trouble," those parasols were hers for as long as she needed to borrow them. They were soon strapped to the top of the sedan.

Her next stop was to the household goods store in Galveston, where she used the credit card she only pulled out for emergencies. She bought three large misting devices with stands and got a price break when she mentioned the Salty Dog being closed for repairs. Those would be delivered in a couple of days. A few other odds and ends and she was ready to launch.

When she arrived at the boardwalk, she hauled the parasols out, and half carried, half dragged them.

"Let me help you with that!" A tall kid rushed out of the store when she passed the Lazy Mazy. "Name's Tanner. A man just doesn't let a woman do the heavy lifting. Shame on Cole."

"He doesn't know I'm here," Valerie snapped, but she wasn't silly enough to refuse his help.

"I heard about Salty Dog. Sad. Really, why wouldn't they just do the repairs? Why wait until there's a huge storm that puts them out of business?"

Valerie really had no time for this, but she talked to Tanner anyway. "I don't know if you have any idea what a good man Cole is."

"Dude, you're starting to sound like my ex-girlfriend."

Oh, now this was interesting. "What do you mean?"

"She had a big crush on Cole."

"I don't know that there's a woman alive who doesn't have a crush on him. Eighteen to eighty. I mean, just the dimples alone, you know?"

"Dimples are just little craters on your cheeks. Big deal. All he did was buy my girlfriend a new waffle cone when hers fell in the sand. She acted like he bought her a car or something! I could have gotten her another cone." He paused. "I just didn't think about it in time."

She glanced over at him. Poor kid looked miserable. "I'm sorry, Tanner."

"What *is* it about that guy?" He stopped walking, not even slightly out of breath from carrying three of the heavy umbrellas over his shoulder.

Valerie stopped, too, to take a deep breath. And to assess this young man, who was tall and muscular. Obviously strong. Definitely good-looking, with blond hair, green eyes and a square jaw.

She didn't have to consider her answer for long. "It's his heart."

He scowled, kept walking, and she kept dragging her one umbrella until they arrived at the Salty Dog. A sign on the front read: Closed for Repairs by the Charming Historical Society.

"Make sure you tell him I helped you with these," Tanner said, putting a damper on his good deed.

"Sure will!" She said in her singsong voice, because he currently reminded her of an oversize third grader.

But before he walked away, Valerie decided she just couldn't let him go without a little advice. She spoke to his retreating back. "Hey, Tanner?"

He turned, hands shoved in his pockets. "Yeah?"

"I assume you have a girlfriend."

He grinned. "Two or three."

"Of course you do." Valerie sighed. "That's your first problem. Pick one. How about your favorite? Pick her. And then always remember that it's the little things, okay? Like having *one* girlfriend and letting her see that she's the only woman in the world for you. Like being the first to get her a new waffle cone when hers drops because you noticed. *Notice*."

"Okay." He nodded and then walked away.

It took Valerie the rest of the afternoon to set up the parasols and string fairy lights outside. The sun was dipping down the horizon and she'd worked up a sweat when she dropped everything to talk to Karen, the manager of The Waterfront. When Valerie asked whether they could share her kitchen for a month until repairs were done, she said for Cole, she'd find a way. Next, Valerie phoned Ava and told her about her plans.

After that, the only thing left to do was text Cole.

Chapter Twenty

Cole spent the day with Max in full-on damage control. Phone calls, one after another. Max had spreadsheets all over Cole's kitchen table, his laptop opened, his mouth set in a scowl.

Nick took the news like a champ, deciding that he would take off for a month and go fishing. Maybe look up that babe he'd hooked up with that one time. But most of their staff did not take the news nearly as well. And Debbie broke Cole's heart.

"I want you to know, sugar, I will be here for you when you're ready to open again. You're the best boss I've ever had."

She had three children and no husband to contribute, so it killed Cole to shut down even for a month. And Lord knew it might even be longer. They couldn't even *start* the renovations until they came up with a down payment. And every day they'd be shut down was another day further in the hole.

Thanks, Dad.

He still hadn't heard from Lloyd, but at this point, Cole felt it best to keep his distance from the man. What he wanted to say to him would best be said with a cooler head.

Late afternoon, he received a text from Valerie: Come to the bar. Ralph has a question for you.

He responded that if Ralph had a question, he should call him, but Valerie insisted this had to be done in person. Either way, he wanted to see her anyway, so he talked Max into taking a break and they drove to the boardwalk.

"What do you think he has to say?" Max pressed. "Could he possibly have any worse news? Why would he have to tell us in person?"

"I don't even want to think about it."

As expected, there wasn't much of a crowd out tonight after yesterday's storm. The sun began its slow dip over the horizon, and streetlights flashed on along the boardwalk. There remained a small group of die-hard amusement park riders, mostly teens, and a few of the storefronts, who'd obviously had no damage, were open and serving.

"Good to know the storm didn't kill everyone's business," Cole muttered.

He stopped cold when he took in the scene before

him. Outside the Salty Dog stood several parasols separated by a few feet and strung with white lights. Valerie was flanked by Ava and Karen.

"What the hell?" Max said. "Is this some kind of lame going-away party? *Not* cool."

Valerie rushed up to Cole and the smile on her face nearly stopped his heart. "I found a solution."

"What kind of a solution?" Max asked, voice dripping with suspicion.

"Now, hear me out," Valerie said, holding out her hands. "You're just locked out of the *inside*. That doesn't mean we can't drag some tables outside and set them up under parasols. I ordered some mist makers so sitting outdoors will be bearable during the day. Ava says that she'll talk to the mayor about any special permits. Of course, we won't have nearly as much room, but we can at least keep one waitress, and our cook."

"Who won't have a kitchen," Cole said, slowly.

"Well, that's where Karen comes in," Valerie said, nodding toward her. "She's offered to share her kitchen with Nick."

Karen bowed. "My kitchen is your kitchen."

Ava piped in. "I know what you're thinking! Who's going to want to sit outside while there's a lot of construction going on right behind them? We can do this model until construction starts, and if or when it gets too noisy and dusty, we'll move y'all into one of the parking lots and cordon it off. That will give you even more room."

"But this is all just temporary, because if you win Mr. Charming, you'll have the money for the deposit to begin the work."

Cole turned to Max, quirking an eyebrow. Max would probably prefer not to pull money out of his IRA with a stiff penalty.

"This could work."

"I think it will!" Valerie squeezed Cole's hands.

"It's an idea," Max said, which in Max-speak meant, "Why didn't I think of that."

"Cole," Valerie said, "can I be the one to call Debbie and let her know she's got her job back?"

His chest felt tight. She'd done this for him, Max and for Debbie, who needed the job. She certainly hadn't done it for herself.

"I've got news for you two," Ava said. "The Mr. Charming contest is down to the two of you now. Tanner called yesterday to drop out of the race."

"You're kidding," Valerie said. "Well, well. He finally realized he didn't have a prayer of beating either one of us, Cole."

"So it's down to you, Cole and Valerie. This contest is yours to win or lose. Congratulations!"

"May the best mister win," Cole said and then with one arm he pulled Valerie into his arms and pressed a kiss against her temple.

Karen smiled, but both Ava and Max didn't know where to look. They took a glance at each other. That seemed to be too much for Ava, who blushed and suddenly got busy with her phone. Max stalked over to the parasols and began inspecting them.

"Do you still work for me?" Cole whispered into her hair.

"I don't think you can afford me," Valerie said, her arms wrapped around his waist. "After this, I'm worth twice my previous rate."

"You *are* invaluable." He pulled her away for privacy and tipped her chin to meet her eyes. "No one's ever done anything like this for me."

"That's because you're always helping everyone else. So it's about time."

"What are you doing tomorrow morning?"

"Sleeping in because I don't have a job."

"Or you could meet me at the lighthouse to surf for a couple of hours. The stretch of beach by the lighthouse is not my favorite spot, but it will do for a beginner like you." He gave her a slow smile.

"Uh-huh. How do you know I haven't spent the last few years becoming an expert?"

He cocked his head. "In Missouri?"

"Fine, I'd love to, but never call me a beginner again."

The next morning, Cole took Sub out for his morning walk, then came back to prep the longboards by waxing each one. He packed coffee and all of his safety equipment. No point in taking chances. Though he was a strong swimmer, he didn't expect the same stamina in the water from Valerie, or any-one else for that matter.

But Valerie had been competitive with him out on the water as well, and this should be fun. Though she'd lived in Missouri and had for years, maybe her jerk of an ex-husband had taken her to California, or Hawaii, and they'd surfed there. By all indications, Valerie hadn't kept up with the sport, but he had no doubt she'd catch on quickly again.

When Valerie arrived in the repaired wagon and parked at the lighthouse, Cole caught her shading her eyes against the already blinding sun and waved her down. And holy shit, she walked toward him wearing a two-piece bikini, a colorful towel wrapped around her waist. He nearly swallowed his tongue.

She went straight into his arms and he held her close against him, relishing her soft flowery scent and gliding his arm down her soft skin.

"Good morning, baby." He handed her a cup of coffee.

"I'm so happy to see you," she said.

"Me, too."

"I was talking to the *coffee*."

"If you weren't holding a hot beverage that might get all over that beautiful smooth skin, I would tackle you to the ground right now."

"Don't let that stop you."

She took a swallow and then set it down on top of the cooler, sliding him the smile that usually hit him right in the knees. This time it hit him a lot further north.

He tackled her, gently, and then they were both on the sandy beach. Him, bracing himself above her.

"I'm also happy to see you." She smiled and kissed him. No gentle kiss. She threaded her fingers through his hair, her tongue hot and insistent, as she drew him deeper into her.

He had to force himself to pull away. "No matter what the movies say, sex on a beach isn't as much fun as it sounds."

She continued to lie splayed on her back, tempting him. Now that the towel had fallen away, he got treated to a view of long, tanned legs.

She went up on her elbows. "Spoken from someone who has experienced this."

"Once," he admitted.

"With your ex-fiancée?"

"Um, no."

"What do you mean, um, no?"

"Because…guess I didn't know her all that well. But I have the feeling that she would have worried too much about breaking a nail."

She sat up straighter. "You didn't really know the woman you were going to *marry*?"

"Okay, I guess it's time we talked about this." He grabbed his own coffee and drank generously.

"I'd say so if there's more to this story. I told you everything about my disaster of a marriage."

"This is…kind of embarrassing."

"More embarrassing than mine? Cole, you're scaring me now, so tell me already." She drew up her legs to her chest and hugged them.

"She was pregnant."

Valerie sucked in a breath and immediately threw her arms around him. "Oh, no. I'm so sorry."

Valerie obviously assumed they'd lost the child. And she'd already shown more compassion than Jessica had after the supposed miscarriage.

Yeah, he was an idiot. "The thing is, I'm sure there never was a baby."

"Why do you think that?"

"We dated a couple of months and she got serious right away. The next thing I know, she's pregnant. It didn't make sense because I've always been so careful, but nothing is a hundred percent effective. So I did the right thing, and I told her we'd get married. She was excited and started to plan our wedding the next day. I should have paid more attention, because she didn't talk much about doctor's appointments. But I was working around the clock, weird shifts. It was a buddy who finally asked me about all this, and I realized I'd never seen an ultrasound. Nothing. When I asked her, she got defensive and said not to worry, that everything was going right along according to schedule. And then one morning she came to me and said she'd had a miscarriage. There'd be no baby, but we should still get married. We could have another baby later on. She didn't seem all that upset. No tears. Nothing. Long story short, I had either been hoodwinked, or she was the coldest woman I've ever known."

Valerie pressed her face to his neck, and he felt a hint of wetness. She was already crying. "You had the decency to believe her. Baby or no baby, *you* thought there was one. You lost something, Cole, even if you never actually did. The dream of a precious baby. I can't imagine how that must have hurt."

The change of perspective would have had any man's head spinning. Valerie had taken this news not only harder than Jessica had, but harder than *he* had. Yes, he'd been bummed he'd lost the chance to prove to be a better father than the one he'd had. To prove to himself he could be a better man even without a good example. But he hadn't been in love with Jessica. The way it had happened left him feeling far too much like Lloyd, which disgusted him.

When he'd pressed to see the ultrasound, Jessica had said there'd be no point now. But he'd never stopped asking. She in turn became more defensive, and increasingly frustrated with his rising doubts. That was when she'd laid down the law: either he stop asking questions, or forget about their marriage.

An easy choice. He would never be the type of man to go along just to keep the peace, asking no questions. And when and if he did become a father, he would be a fully involved one.

"I did realize then how much I want a child. A family."

"You're a good man." She framed his face, her eyes glimmering with tears.

Funny thing was he'd never thought that about himself. A better man wouldn't have found himself in a complication with someone he didn't love. He'd been lonely and didn't do the abstinence thing well. Not that he hadn't tried, and to be fair, he'd done okay for the past year. Until Valerie.

He stood and offered Valerie his hand. "It's too early in the day to cry."

She wiped away tears with the pads of her fingers. "I'm sorry. I'm a soft touch."

"You always have been, and I think that's probably why I fell in love with you."

"Cole," she said on such a light whisper that he almost missed it over the break of a wave. "I'm falling in love with you all over again. And it scares me."

"I know. It will be different this time." He squeezed her hand.

They'd always had the most incredible way of segueing from teasing each other to quiet words. And back again. He'd never felt this way about any other woman before, never this intensity that balanced with the ease of friendship and trust.

He tugged at a lock of her hair. "Are you ready to surf?"

"We're really going to surf?" she sniffed. "I thought you got me out here to make out."

"That, too." He walked over to the longboard he'd

chosen for her to use today. "How long has it really been since you surfed?"

She seemed to consider it, looking at him from under lowered eyelids, biting at her lower lip in that adorable way of hers. "Take the last time I saw you and subtract a day."

"I bet you take to it again like you did before."

Still, he attached an ankle rope to her board, then squatted below her and attached the brace to her ankle. He took his time gliding his hand over her soft leg, enjoying the contact.

She ruffled his hair as he crouched below her, strapping the Velcro that secured the ankle brace. "Look at this hair."

"I need a haircut."

"Please don't. I love your long hair."

He stood, meeting her gaze. "The strap is just so you don't lose the board out there. I don't want you worrying about that. It's also less likely to hit your head if you wipe out."

"You always looked out for me."

He'd purposely taken her to a beach for beginners, not that he would tell her that. Here, they'd surf in the white water of the low breaks to get her used to it again. Later, he could see taking her along to the beach that he and Max frequented.

After a few reminders, he took her hand and together they walked to the surf, Sub following behind. He always stopped in about a foot of water, and Cole never had to worry about him.

"We won't go too far out this time," he said.

They both took to the boards, paddling out past the break of the waves.

"C'mon, Cole, this is baby stuff," Valerie said a minute later. "I can do better."

"I know you can. Just do me a favor and let's try this first. It's been a while, yeah?"

"Not for you."

"I don't mind."

She watched him wait for the small white wave as it curled toward the shore, then raising his torso, he hopped on with those long, muscular legs. He was grace in motion, an Adonis out on the water, honey hair with natural sun-bleached highlights people paid good money for. This was too easy for him, but she loved that he wanted her to be safe. He could have taken her to a different beach and watched as she wiped out over and over again.

Still, she teased him as he balanced on his board. "Show-off."

"Let me see what you can do," he said, swimming over to her.

"Just watch this." Determined to be a part of something that meant so much to him, she paddled out and emulated him. "It's like riding a bicycle."

Wait for the wave. Catch it.

Brace your arms on the board and hop on.

Ride the wave.

Sounded easy enough, but she missed the wave

the first time because timing was everything. Surfing, so much like life. Who would have thought? The third time she caught her groove and didn't *completely* wipe out when she fell. She did come up sputtering water and feeling like a real newbie. This was what she got for giving up on the sport that had brought her so much joy in her youth. Every time she'd come to Charming for a quick visit with Gram, she stayed away from the surf. Too many raw memories. Cole hadn't been in Charming then and without him the town was simply a place to visit Gram and nothing more. Those tender memories were back with her now, wrapping themselves around her heart like seaweed.

"Are you okay?" Cole waded over to her. He wore the start of a dimpled smile.

How she loved that face.

"I'm good." Her board floated nearby, still attached to her by the rope. She shook stray hairs out of her face.

Her stinking pride would not allow her to say that her leg hurt a little from the fall. She'd ice it later and join Gram in the aches and pains department. But like he didn't quite believe her, Cole was at her side, his hands around her waist. Even in this warm water, she shivered at his touch.

"I should check."

"I think you should."

His hands lowered to her butt, squeezing, and with a smile he went down one leg, gliding down her thigh, her knee and finally down to her ankle. "All good here."

"It's the other leg." She smirked.

"Likely story." He touched her knee and she winced. "We better ice this, baby."

"Really? We're done here? Already?"

"It's time for the make-out portion of the morning. You did good for your first time back on a board. This is just the beginning."

There seemed to be a deeper meaning to his words. She wanted to believe him, to know that this connection they had between them would never wane, never get squashed by time and obligations. Responsibilities. She loved this little world they'd created, just the two of them. It was a peek into a simpler time of her life. A time without doubts and fears. A time when her life stretched before her, and she trusted herself and the decisions she would make. She'd made a lot of mistakes, but Cole had never been one of them.

While he gathered the boards and everything he'd brought, she came up behind him, curling her arms around his waist. She pressed a wet kiss to his back, his golden skin tasting like coconut. He turned and dropped the boards, and, hand on the nape of her neck, tugged her close for a deep and heartfelt kiss. With so little clothing between them, it became easy to get worked up fast. His thumb moved aside the cup of her bikini, rubbed and tweaked her nipple. She moaned into his mouth.

"Let's go," he said, practically taking off at a run.

Valerie followed Cole as he jogged back to the lighthouse, Sub happily ahead of them. Tossing the boards to the side by the front door, they rushed inside. She ran up the winding staircase behind him, the same steps that she'd so tentatively taken not long ago. Then, she'd been worried about the strength of her emotions for him. Not trusting they could have whatever they'd had once before. And truthfully, they didn't have that. They had something new. Something fresh and sparkling and promising. Hopeful. There was just no other word for this feeling.

She caught a very quick glance at Cole's bedroom, figuring she'd notice all the furnishings and decor later. Much later. Swim clothes were discarded and flew in every direction. Her bikini bottoms wound up on a lampshade, she noticed lazily. She lay flat on her back, on Cole's surprisingly soft blue cotton sheets. She kissed him, each kiss deeper and hotter, wilder, her hands all over him.

"Hey." Cole braced himself above her and with his heartbreakingly beautiful, slow smile, tipped her chin to meet his eyes. "I love you."

Those tender words slid into her with a sharp and sweet ache. "I love you."

It had been too long since she'd meant those three words. So long, that now she couldn't stop saying them.

"I love you, Cole. I love you, I love you," she said, as he kissed from the column of her neck, sliding lower, and lower still, teasing and tasting every sensitive point along the way.

This time, when he slid into her, the feeling was both delicious and electric as they found their rhythm.

Chapter Twenty-One

"I should go home to make sure my father and grandmother haven't killed each other."

But she was enjoying lying in Cole's arms too much and her comment was more of a general observation. Like when she thought of deep cleaning the house until the feeling passed.

I should really clean today. Maybe vacuum. Those windows look dirty. Ah, never mind. I'm going to read a book.

"Just a little while longer," Cole said, tugging her tighter.

Outside the bedroom, Sub scratched at the door, then apparently gave up and went to do something else.

After their second time making love, in which

Cole had apparently gone for a personal best, trying to beat her personal best, she'd finally taken the time to check out the bedroom. Neat and orderly, it was tastefully decorated in the home's nautical theme. The lamp that had caught her bikini seemed to be the figure of a lighthouse. This entire house had probably been decorated by the landlord, but Cole's personal touches were everywhere. Her gaze gravitated to those, wondering what they would tell her.

Another longboard stood in a corner of the room. A couple of retired ones hung on the wall, mounted like decorations. A shelf with books. There were photos of waves crashing against rocks. Photos of Cole with friends. An older one of Angela and him. Cole looked younger, proudly dressed in his navy blues, smiling, his arm around Angela.

She caught more photos of surfers on the crest of huge waves, another of... Her heart stopped. She recognized *this* photo. The one she'd taken of Cole, the one that had won an award.

"My photo!" She came up on her elbows. "You kept it."

"Of course. You gave it to me and it's the best photo ever taken of me. How could I let *that* go?"

"It's a photo of your back. That can't be the best photo ever taken of you."

"What do you mean? I have a nice backside, don't I?" He winked. "C'mon, baby, *you* took this photo. It's damn good."

But she would have expected this photo to be in a

box somewhere, along with other memories. If he'd even managed to hang on to it after all these years. It had occurred to her that it might have been with Angela for years, and during Cole's many travels. And then, eventually, back again with him. Tears sprang in her eyes and she swallowed at the tightness in her throat.

No one had ever made her feel as special as Cole did.

"You *kept* it."

Not only kept it but given it practically a place of honor among all his other photos. For the first time in a long while, Valerie recalled the feeling she'd had when she took that photo. The way she'd known from that moment that the shot would be exceptional. Like the opportunity had been gifted—the subject matter, setting and lighting. But she couldn't discount her own ability to visualize and conceptualize. She'd just somehow forgotten.

"Why did you stop taking photos?"

"I got busy, and it's not practical. Like you said, that's no way to make a living."

So she'd chosen the safe route. She couldn't regret that, because being able to support herself meant she'd been independent enough to walk away from a marriage that had practically killed her spirit.

His hand skimmed down her back. "I thought you should get an education first, but I believed in you."

"I know. Maybe you're the only one who ever did."

He pulled her to him, her back to his front, nuzzling her shoulder. "I doubt that. When are you going to start up again?"

"Taking photos? I don't know. I took a few of the sunset the other night, after the storm. With my phone camera." She chuckled softly. "Things have changed quite a bit in the world of photography in fourteen years."

They were both quiet for a moment, and then Cole rose from the bed, pulling her up with him. "Let's eat."

"You're going to feed me, too?"

"My cooking skills are still sadly lacking, but I make some amazing scrambled eggs."

He pulled on a pair of board shorts and she found one of his T-shirts. They came down the staircase a lot slower this time. As Cole poured orange juice and cracked eggs, an air of domesticity settled around them. The difference being, for her, they couldn't really keep their hands off each other. Cole had pulled her between his legs, and they lay on the couch eating straight out of the pan.

Sub sat at attention, silently begging for a nibble with doe-like eyes.

"What's going on with your father and grandmother?" Cole said.

"He dropped in on us unexpectedly. Neither of us expected him. He and Gram don't get along since my parents' divorce. Gram actually took my mother's side."

"Ouch. His own mother, huh?"

"I know she loves him, but boy, is she tough. That's her only child. He disappointed her and she's never let him forget it."

"That must be hard." He played with her hair and she wondered if he was remembering Angela.

He'd never say it out loud, but no doubt he pictured what he'd do for another day with his mother. If he'd had a chance, he would have taken her on his board at sunset, just like Mr. Finch's wife. She had to swallow at the sudden tightness in her throat.

"It's ridiculous," she said, shaking it off. "I don't say this often, but my grandmother is wrong. They still have each other, and every day they spend angry is another day they lose."

"Yeah," he said softly, and she knew that her words had hit home.

She turned in his arms, reaching to thread her fingers in his beautiful hair. "I love you."

He slid her a lazy smile and tugged on a lock of her hair.

"And now I really have to take a shower. My old boss might need my help later. He's really incapable of doing anything without me. Get this. He thinks he can win Mr. Charming!"

"You think you're funny." He chased her to the shower.

"I'm really going now." Valerie breathed heavily against the shower stall.

Cole's handprint remained on the steamy glass

wall, evidence of all the clean fun they'd just had in there. And he was right about the pulse setting.

He slapped her butt as she opened the stall door. She toweled off, trying to tame her wet hair, and gave one last longing look at Cole's naked body. His sinewy back was to her, two hands braced against the wall as he dipped his head under the nozzle.

"Either stop staring or get back in here," he said.

"Okay, okay. I'm going." She laughed.

She found her bikini top on the floor, pulled the bottoms off the lighthouse lamp and grabbed her keys.

Sub sat at the bottom of the steps, sunning himself under a ray of sunlight splashing through the windows. This home was like a sailor's dream, and Valerie felt like she'd been walking in one for weeks. After her heartbreak, she'd never imagined she could feel such joy again. But this was what happened when a woman had a second chance. This was what happened with a little bit of courage. Now she was more powerful than she'd ever been when she'd tried to fix a marriage that couldn't be fixed.

"Bye, Sub. I'll see you later." Valerie swung the front door open and walked to her father's rental car.

Her phone buzzed in her tote bag and she pulled it out to check the caller ID. Greg.

Reluctantly, she picked it up because she'd been ignoring his calls. She hadn't seen the need to further rehash their stalemate. Any other time, she might have tried to reason with him.

"Yes?"

"All right, Valerie, you've worn me down."

Worn him down? They hadn't spoken since he showed up in Charming like a wart.

"What do you want?"

"I'll sell the house."

"Oh, that's nice. Considering, you know, this was part of our divorce settlement. I'm guessing your attorney gave you the bad news?"

"No, this is all me. We were friends once, and I think we should end the same way. I could take you to court again, arguing that since Regina's now pregnant, it makes sense to stay in a better school district. I'd probably win."

Greg droned on and on. The news of Regina's pregnancy was hardly a blip on Valerie's radar. Valerie had wanted children, but Greg had said not yet. Another way to control Valerie, she had to assume. She'd respected his wishes, assuming he'd eventually change his mind. Now she was grateful beyond measure that this jerk would never be the father of *her* children.

"Regina found a larger home for us, still in the same district, but we need to jump on it. We put an offer in contingent on the sale of this home."

"Thank you for reconsidering. This means so much to me. I could use that money to start over. I'm staying in Texas."

"I assumed that." Greg cleared his throat. "When will you be here to sign the papers?"

"Can't we do this through the mail or fax?"

"We could, but I'd like you to come home. It's my only condition to selling now without any more delays."

"Why?" Just one last hurrah at controlling her, she had to assume.

"Do you have to question everything?" His tone sounded agitated and Valerie wondered what was going on.

"I'll sign the documents. It seems easier to do this through the mail. That's what overnight express is all about."

"It's the only way I'll do this. Do you want to sell the house or *not*?"

Clearly, he wasn't done controlling her but if she could finally be free of him by taking a quick trip back to Missouri, it would be well worth her time and effort. She would have to go back at some point anyway and box up the rest of her things from the apartment. She'd say goodbye to her colleagues in person. Have one last lunch with Ann Marie.

If she indulged Greg this one last time, then she'd be free of him forever when their house sold.

Since she'd be thousands of miles away from him, he'd understand he'd lost the war. Knowing he'd won this small battle, getting her to come back, she had a difficult time saying her next words through clenched teeth.

"Sure. We'll do it your way. I'll be out in a few days."

"Let me know when, and I'll pick you up at the airport."

Valerie put her phone away and drove back to the mobile home park, a throb of guilt pulsing like a knot in her forehead.

"I hope I am driving with the angels, because I don't feel like much of a saint right now," she muttered.

Greg thought he had won. This time, though, she'd allowed him to win. This could work for her. She'd go back to Missouri, and get the house sold like she'd wanted all this time. No more holding out the carrot stick and then yanking it back. No more threatening to drag him back into court.

She drove back to her grandmother's home. At the door, Valerie immediately froze at the sound of Gram inside…crying? Oh, no! What now? In the next instance she opened the door, and one thing became abundantly clear: Gram was…*laughing.*

"The ball flew straight through the window of his kitchen. I still remember him standing at our front door, saying, 'What is *this*?' And your papi said, 'Don't you recognize a baseball when you see it?'"

"I was in so much trouble," Dad said, laughing, too.

Valerie's hand stayed on the doorknob, and she stealthily backed out of the house and shut the door. She had to leave these two alone. Last night, voices were raised in anger, and today…today they were *laughing.*

Valerie headed to the beach instead. She parked at the boardwalk, heaved her tote bag and wound up at the Lazy Mazy Kettle Corn store. She'd avoided this storefront but if ever there was a day to indulge, this was it. She wrapped the towel around her waist and walked inside.

"Hey, there. Look what the cat dragged in."

"I'll take a ten-pound bag, please."

"Of course, darlin'." Tanner smiled and winked. "Ten-pound bag, comin' right up."

"I heard you dropped out of Mr. Charming."

"Don't have to win some stupid Mr. Charming contest to know that I'm the bomb-diggity." He shoveled popcorn into a bag. "Besides, my girlfriend got jealous of all the attention."

"Didn't think you could beat Cole, huh?"

"Yeah, Cole." Tanner snorted. "I could have beat him with my hands tied behind my back. My hands tied behind my back and my legs bound, too."

It took everything in her not to roll her eyes. They were back to that again. And yet there was something unnerving about Tanner. He was handsome, young and clueless. He reminded her in some ways of a younger Cole. And then pain sliced through her at the memory of that sweet boy, before he'd lost so much. He still managed to put on a smile, flirt and somehow be happy.

Tanner tied the end of the two-foot-long bag and handed it to her. "I forgot to tell you. I'm rooting for you to win Mr. Charming. I totally approve, dude."

"Except that I'm not a *dude*, Tanner. That's the point."

Tanner gave her a thumbs-up. "Totally noticed you're not a dude."

"And stop saying *totally*!" Clutching her bag of popcorn, Valerie left the store and went to find a quiet place to sit for a few minutes and wait.

When Valerie got home an hour later, Gram and Dad were sitting and watching TV.

"Hey, sugar," Gram said. "I heard about the Salty Dog. Lois told me."

"Yep, I lost my job."

"I'm sorry," Gram said.

"No worries. Tonight, they'll announce the winner of the Mr. Charming contest, and I'll find out if I won."

"Mami told me all about it," her father said. "Good for you."

That was the last thing she'd expected to hear from her father, but it felt oddly gratifying to have his support.

"I probably won't win but it's been fun."

She changed into jeans and a T-shirt, and because a few important items needed to be discussed, Valerie took her father aside while Gram continued to watch TV.

"I've got to go back to Missouri in a couple of days. Is there any possible way you could stay a little longer?"

"I can try and work something out. Don't worry."

"She's getting to where she'll be okay on her own soon, and Lois can help, too. But I think if you stayed...that would be good."

He smiled and there was a flicker of gratitude in his gaze. "Got it. Anything else I can do to help?"

"Um, the reason you're here?"

"Right. It's all been paid. I walked down to the office this morning and handed them a check. Taken care of."

Like the air had been let out of her, Valerie sagged in relief. Literally. "Thank you. What did she say?"

"I reminded her that my father left a small sum of money with me, to take care of these kinds of issues should they ever arise unexpectedly. He was prepared."

"Oh my goodness. He *did*?"

"No." Her father shoved his hands in the pockets of his dockers and tipped back on his heels. "But I do know my mother."

"You're an evil genius, aren't you?"

"I have my moments. It might be too late, but I've started the financial education. However, I'd feel better if I just took the reins."

"It might be best at this point," Valerie admitted. "She's too used to being taken care of."

It was one more example of why Valerie had never and *would* never depend on a man for her survival. From the moment she'd graduated from college, she'd been on a path of independence and that had never waned. Greg used to say, 'You don't need me, do you?' To which she'd replied, 'I'm not *supposed* to need you.' But he'd also said, 'I feel like I'm your roommate. All you need is my half of the rent.'"

He hadn't been all that wrong, in hindsight. It had been different in the beginning, but she'd emotionally checked out of her marriage long before it was officially over. Long before his affair. That didn't make infidelity in any way excusable, but she could see now why someone like Regina had been exactly what Greg needed.

"I told her about Savannah." He lowered his head.

"And what's the verdict on that?" Valerie nudged her chin in the direction of the room in which Gram sat watching TV.

"We landed on the positive side. So there's that."

Right. Another marriage failure, but at least this time, his mother approved. Probably harbored some fantasy that Dad and Valerie's mother would eventually reconcile. Not likely, since infidelity was almost impossible to recover from.

She ought to know.

He met her eyes. "Do you…think your mother would give me another chance? I was such an idiot, but I still love her."

"I'm sorry, but I don't think so."

She took his hands in hers, because she did feel sad for him. Her poor hapless father, who'd once loved Valerie's mother, and then presumably, he'd loved Savannah. But relationships starting with infidelity rarely lasted. The statistics relating to second marriages born out of them told the true story. She supposed that was the way Regina and Greg's marriage would go, if they even made it to the altar. This time she wished them well, with zero bitterness, which meant she'd truly moved on.

Chapter Twenty-Two

Tonight, the announcement of the winner of Mr. Charming would take place on the boardwalk. Signs led those who were interested to the raised platform set up in advance on the beach where a country band would perform this Saturday. Ava had decided to take full advantage of the opportunity to call even more attention to the contest, and had a PA system set up so that everyone on the boardwalk could hear the results.

And in true Ava fashion, she'd hired the local high school marching band to open the festivities.

"She doesn't do anything halfway," Valerie muttered.

She stood in the new outside dining area of the

Salty Dog under the partial shade of a parasol. Every table was full.

Debbie came behind Valerie, holding her tray. "Reminds me of someone else I know."

"Who, me?" Valerie deadpanned.

She had to agree, though, that she and Ava had a great deal in common. They could be good friends someday.

"And thank you, really, for saving my job. You're brilliant."

"No." Valerie shrugged. "Just a teacher who's had to make do with whatever was available at the moment. You'd be surprised how willing others are to help if you'll just ask."

"You gave everything to this contest, girl, and I for one think you're going to win it."

"Thanks, but for the first time in my life, I don't want to win."

Debbie gave her a quizzical look, scrunching up her nose. "How's that?"

"I know, right? But he *deserves* to win."

"Well, I don't know about that. He's a Mr., sure, but—"

Valerie glanced over to him now, laughing with Max, and chatting with some of their diners. When he caught her gaze, he winked and sent her a slow smile. Her heart tugged in a powerful ache. *He* was the real deal. The actual Mr. Charming. Appealing. Electrifying and charismatic.

And now she truly believed that he was hers. They

were going to work. She believed this with every breath she took.

After the marching band did their thing, Ava walked up to the podium, a photographer close behind. He held one of those big funny checks, flipped the other way.

"Everyone, we have our results!" she said over the microphone.

Here we go.

Someone whistled, and the crowd became far more subdued. There were whispers and hushed words here and there, rolling through the crowd. She'd never in her life wanted to lose more than at this moment. Cole deserved this. He and Max needed it now far more than she did.

"Y'all, it was so close that only ten votes separate the winner from the loser! *Ten!* Can you believe it?"

"Tell us already," a man said. "We want to know if our Mr. Charming pees standing up."

There was a roar of laughter, which hushed when Ava sent the man a censuring look. Lips pursed, eyebrow quirked, she appeared to be every bit the socialite.

"You know, I admit at first I didn't like the idea. Lord knows we get stuck in our ways here in Charming. But it grew on me."

Oh no. Oh no, no, no. Did that mean *she'd* won? She couldn't win! Could she forfeit? Could she give the money to Cole without taking away his man card?

Would he even take it? Curse her stupid competitive spirit!

"…Mr. Charming… Cole Kinsella," Ava announced.

The applause was deafening, and Valerie's heart resumed its regular rhythm.

"That's what I'm talking about," said one man, standing.

"How about that. Life makes sense again," said another. Then he grunted when a woman elbowed him.

Cole ran up the steps of the scaffold and Ava flipped the check to reveal his name.

"Congratulations, Cole."

"Hey, thanks to everyone who voted for me. As you know, I had some stiff competition this year." He pointed to Valerie in the crowd. "This is the first year I entered this contest, and it's also the first year Mr. Charming had a formidable opponent. Just the voting tells you that story. I won by a hair, so I feel like I should share this with my opponent. C'mon up, baby."

Valerie shook her head and waved her hands no, but Debbie pushed her toward the stage.

Cole draped his arm around Valerie's waist.

"It took an outsider to Charming to challenge us, because as Ava said, we can get stuck in our ways. I propose that next year, we open up the contest to everyone. And the purse can be split in half, because that's what I'm doing tonight."

Valerie smiled up at him, wondering if she looked as adoring as Ava had that first day when Cole had talked her into changing the rules of the contest. Not because he had any other agenda but giving her a chance. She loved him so much.

Ava took the microphone back. "Well said. Everyone, please visit all of our vendors tonight and show your love with your wallets. In addition to our bar and grill, the Salty Dog, we also have fine dining at The Waterfront, the Lazy Mazy Kettle Corn…"

Phones were taken out of purses and pockets, and the photographer took one shot after another of Cole. Holding the plaque. Cole and Ava with the large check, as she handed it to him. Cole with Max, who'd come up to the stage at some point. And of course, most of the photos were of Valerie and Cole.

The repairs on the Salty Dog could get started now. Some people were kind, too, telling Valerie she should have won and that they'd voted for her. Others giving her a thumbs-up simply for entering because she'd made an old Charming tradition interesting.

When they walked off the stage, Cole was greeted with handshakes and in the crowd, they got separated. He looked behind and beckoned her to him, knowing the crowd would part for her. But she wanted him to have this time and appreciate his win.

She took in a deep, cleansing breath of the salty-sweet air. Kids passed by holding waffle cones and pink cotton candy. The delicious smell of kettle corn hung in the air. The Ferris wheel had a line, and there were the fools who risked life and limb on the glider just to save a little bit of time in getting across the boardwalk. Tonight, she had nothing *but* time, so she strolled among the crowds of mostly young couples and teens who were out past sunset.

Taking the steps down a short viewing pier, she walked to the edge, bracing her arms against the rail, and listened to the waves. She felt calm and peaceful to the seat of her soul.

"Valerie."

She turned. "Hi, baby."

Cole joined her, pulling her in close, her back to his front. "Ten votes. That's all it took to win this."

"And I'm not going to take half of that money. It was sweet, and I love you, but I want all of it to go toward the renovations."

He bent his head to kiss her neck. "Whatever you say."

"Oh, I like when you're this cooperative." She was only a little bit nervous about what she had to tell him next because she hoped Cole, of all people, would understand. She turned in his arms to face him. "Next week, I need to go back to Missouri."

At his stunned expression, she shook her head and kept talking. "Just for a day or so. Get this. Greg called, and he's changed his mind about selling the house. His only condition is that I come out so we can sign all the papers."

"Okay. I'll go with you. I should be able to take some time off now. Max owes me."

She considered it for a moment. Cole could meet her friends, see where she used to work. But Greg would *hate* it. He'd make life even more difficult when he confirmed that she'd moved on with Cole. She didn't want to be a sore winner. This might even make Greg reconsider, throw up some other obstacle. She just didn't wholly trust him. But after two years of this mess, they seemed close to selling. Greg had sounded highly motivated.

"No. That won't work. Greg… I told him about you. He's always known about our history. If he sees you, he's just going to know that we're together again."

"So *what*?"

"I can't risk anything going wrong with this. He's agreed, and if he sees you…he'll find one more way to screw me. He'll be jealous."

She shouldn't care, but Greg held all the cards right now. If she had to humor him one last time, she'd do it.

"Jealous? The man who cheated on you? Valerie, why do you care what he thinks?"

"I *don't*. But he can delay the sale of our house again, force me back to court, anything he wants. If you're there, it's as if I'm pouring gasoline on fire."

"Go back and sell the house, like you have to, but stop jumping through hoops for this man. Is he still controlling you?"

"That's what he *thinks* he's doing but this will work in my favor. Greg has moved on and so have I."

"Have you? Or are you still wondering whether you should stay here with me?"

"What? Don't be ridiculous. I love you, and I want us to work. I'm going to stay in Charming."

"That's not what this looks like."

"I am coming back, even though there are absolutely no guarantees for me. It's a risk." She waved her hands between them. "We're a risk."

He blinked and she caught a glimmer of hurt in his gaze. "I don't see it that way. The way I see it, *this* is the rest of my life. And I don't take it lightly."

"Neither do I." She bit her lower lip, feeling guilt press down.

It might look like she was choosing Greg over Cole right now, but of course she wasn't. She was simply trying to win and winning for now meant playing the game Greg's way. Cole would have to understand. Last she checked, he didn't like losing, either. "This is oddly familiar. You, leaving at the end of summer. It's about that time, isn't it?"

"It's not like that. You had to know I'd go back to get the rest of my things and move here officially. This is just happening a little sooner than I planned."

"When I pictured you going back, I thought we'd do it together."

"So did I, but then this came up and I just don't

want to blow my chance to get this over with once and for all."

"Valerie, look at me." He tipped her chin. "I know what I want. I always have. It's not some great mystery. I pick you, every single day, but I need you to pick me, too. I can't do this alone. I need you to be in, all the way in. Like I am."

"I am! I'll be back in a few days. You can't go with me, not this time, but please don't make this a thing."

"It's your decision. Maybe this wasn't going to work anyway."

"Don't say that, Cole."

"Sounds like your mind is made up. Whether you realize it or not, you're making a choice. If this is what you want, Valerie, you won't hear me beg." His voice had a clipped edge and he turned and slowly walked down the pier and away from her.

"Cole!" she shouted but he kept walking.

And she *refused* to run after him and throw herself at his feet. He wasn't going to beg, and, well, neither was she! He was being incredibly unreasonable and if he was really going to end them over something this stupid, she was better off.

Except that no burden had been lightened. Instead, she felt horribly gutted. Slayed.

Men! Just, men! Why couldn't he understand she needed to cooperate with Greg to finally get her way? She wasn't doing anything wrong. She wasn't abandoning Cole. She didn't love Greg, hadn't for a long time.

Her heart cracked open like a walnut. Cole wasn't wrong about one thing. She was having a difficult time letting go of this battle she'd had with Greg over a stupid house.

Chapter Twenty-Three

For the next few days Cole spent more than his normal amount of time on the surf. Evenings he hung out with Max and Sub. The Salty Dog was serving food only, no liquor, but that was going well so far, and would keep them afloat in addition to the contest money.

Sub whined.

"Yeah, I miss her, too," Cole said, giving him a piece of bacon.

"Would you two *stop* feeling sorry for yourselves?" Max demanded from the couch where he sat, legs crossed at the ankles, watching the game. "You don't see me walking around moaning and groaning."

"Why would you be?"

"Because Valerie was good for business." Max slid him a look from under narrowed lids. "She's got ideas that I can't dream up. It's that burst of creativity that completely eludes me. How long will she be gone?"

"I have no idea."

"You mean you didn't *ask*?"

"She's leaving, and I asked her not to leave."

"Did you ask nicely?"

"No, I didn't ask *nicely*. I told her she had to make a choice between me and that turd of an ex-husband."

"Great. You're jealous of the man. For someone so smart, you're pretty damn stupid." Max crossed his arms behind his neck. "So you gave her an ultimatum? Those always go over so well. I know I like them. How about you?"

"I didn't give her an ultimatum. But I need to know that she's not going to run off every time that loser asks."

"Because you have abandonment issues?"

"Damn you." Cole threw a bottle cap at Max.

Max laughed. "Hey, I hear what you're not saying. Coming from our situation, and how we lived for several years, it makes total sense. We always had each other's six. The people who never abandoned you were part of our team. Brothers. But Valerie *wasn't* a SEAL and she hasn't been trained the way we were. We've had to let some of that go in the civilian world. Not everyone has been through rescues that require us to form one cohesive unit that never questions or alters the plan. It sounds like Valerie altered your plan and you hate that."

Max wasn't wrong.

He'd been through rough terrain, not to mention seas, but this was different. And he'd rather go through a minefield. Hell, no doubt about it. At least he could understand the thought pattern behind minefields. Expect anything.

With Valerie, he couldn't help but feel abandoned again. And this time, he'd been blindsided.

It was now four days since Cole had last seen Valerie.

Every summer he'd simply accepted her leaving, knowing she had to go. This time, he'd been the first to walk away before he could be left behind. It might be irrational, but he feared that if Valerie left Charming, she might not come back.

Cole had now been through far worse than Valerie Villanueva and survived. He'd been abandoned before. By a deadbeat father, by his mother through no fault of her own, by a lying fiancée and by Valerie every single summer of his youth.

Yeah, he'd be okay, even if for the past few days his heart was little more than a raw nerve ending that beat out of force of habit.

Cole sat next to Max with a cold beer. He needed to get away from this place and clear his head. Charming was a great town for everyone else to relax and unwind. Him, not so much.

"Is that cabin your friend owned in Hill Country still available?" Cole asked.

Maybe if he did some fishing and got back down to basics. Spent some time alone to clear his head.

"Sure is. You're thinking of taking off?"

With their temporary new business model, he wasn't as needed on the premises and wouldn't be for at least a month.

"Seems like I could get away. Might be the best time."

"Whatever it takes to get you back on track. I need you firing on all cylinders, Mr. Charming."

Ten thousand dollars notwithstanding, Cole wasn't a fan of that nickname. He was hardly living up to the title lately.

Cole gave Sub a pat. "Sub and I will take a few days, and when we get back, we'll hit the ground running."

The doorbell rang and Cole went to open the door to find Lloyd there. On the good news front, at least he looked sober. On the bad news front, Cole had nothing to say to him.

"Can I come in, son?"

Max brushed by them both. "I'm taking Sub for a walk. Let's go, boy."

One didn't have to ask Sub twice and off they went. "Sure, come in."

Lloyd walked in and, as most people did, spent several minutes in awe of his surroundings. "This... wow. I'm glad you get to live here."

He felt a twinge of guilt that he'd never invited Lloyd over before, but that was gone quickly when he remembered the roof at the Salty Dog. Cole nearly asked him if he wanted a beer, then stopped himself. He'd always taken for granted that drinking was a social activity, but some people, Lloyd being one of them, couldn't drink at all. And Cole would not offer him a chance again. Not in his home, and not at his bar.

"Where have you been?" Cole led him to the great room where he nodded at the couch. "Haven't seen you around much lately."

"You haven't been by the apartment and you asked me to stay away from the bar."

"I told you to stop drinking."

"That's the same thing for me."

Cole nodded. "You may not have heard the latest. That last storm was too much for that old roof to take. The Historical Society shut us down."

Lloyd had the decency to lower his head. "I heard. And I'm sorry."

"We're going to be okay. The work has already started."

"Yeah, well, that's why I'm here. I wanted to do my part." He reached into his back pocket. "You may not remember that I play a pretty mean game of twenty-one."

Cole tamped down his temper, but it still flashed. "You've been gambling?"

"It's the only way I thought I could help."

"I didn't need your help."

"I know you don't. You never did. Some boys don't do well when they grow up without a father, but—"

"I had a great mother. She more than made up for you."

If the words sounded cold and callous, Cole was over it. He'd tried to be his mother's son but some people looked at kindness as weakness. Like Lloyd.

"That's true. I've been ashamed for a long time for what I did to you and Angela. Truth is, I don't deserve a son like you, and I know it." He handed Cole the check.

Out of pure curiosity, Cole accepted the check, and almost laughed at the amount.

"It's not much but it's all I had left. I came with four hundred dollars and left with two hundred. I guess that's a pretty good metaphor for my life." He slowly shook his head.

"I can't take this. You need it more than I do." He tried to hand it back to Lloyd, but he held up his palm.

"Just let me do this one thing for you. I haven't done much else, you have to admit. Honestly, when we first met, I thought maybe we might be something alike. That we'd get along and could be pals since I'd obviously missed my chance at being a real father. When I saw you with people and behind the bar, a natural born charmer, I thought, hey, that's me. He's a chip off the old block."

Every muscle in Cole tensed to granite. But he'd let the old man believe what he wanted. Cole knew the truth.

"Now I see how different we are." Lloyd went on and his voice broke. "You're a solid guy. The real deal. And you remind me so much of Angela."

"Thanks." It was the highest compliment the old man could ever give Cole.

Lloyd stood. "You don't have to believe me, and I wouldn't blame you. But I started a twelve-step program. I'm going to be less of a burden on you and more of a help."

From what he understood, twelve-step programs didn't work unless a person worked on them. He didn't see Lloyd doing that, but at least the sentiment was in the right direction.

"Just take care of yourself and that will be more than enough for me."

Later that night, Cole packed an overnight bag for his trip to the cabin. With every item he threw in, he thought of another Valerie-infused regret.

Signing up for the Navy without telling Valerie, but simply blindsiding her with the information at the last possible minute. Blowing up their plans and expecting her to understand.

Not looking her up when he'd come back stateside.

Not telling her on the first day he saw her again that he'd never stopped loving her.

Being the first to walk away.

Sub whined and wagged his tail.

"You have it so easy," Cole said, shaking his head.

He regretted giving her an ultimatum. It had been stupid. Immature. He regretted having too much pride to accept that the best way he could help her was to stay behind. After all, now, as in then, Valerie had always been a loyal friend, too. He trusted her as much as he loved her.

Without her, the Salty Dog wouldn't be operating. She'd gone out of her way, finding a solution to keep them open during the roof repairs. And though she needed money, too, she'd suggested Debbie take the one waitress job they'd have available during repairs. She'd also gone so far as to suggest dropping out of the contest so that he and Max would have the money for the bar. She'd *shown* him in many ways that she loved him. That she'd do anything for him.

And he'd thrown it all away.

Valerie hadn't left town, and even in the fog of sadness that ripped through her, she realized something true. For too long, she'd let fear guide most of her choices. She'd tried for all of her adult life not to need anyone, seeing that as nothing but a weakness.

Now she saw there could be a reason to need someone in all the right ways.

And she needed Cole. Needed him so much that she ached without him.

And she understood what she had to do. For possibly the first time in her life, she'd stop fighting. Sometimes, that was the only way to win.

Greg picked up. "Hey, Val. When will you be arriving? I've been waiting to make the appointment with the Realtor until you confirm."

"I'm not coming."

"Why not? We need to discuss how we're going to sell the house. Some improvements would get us a better price, for instance. But of course, that requires an investment."

Ah. So, this was his new angle. No wonder he'd wanted her to come back. Probably wanted to show her all the things that needed fixing in the house she hadn't lived in for two years. More delays. And a trip would have been a total waste of her time.

"And I'm guessing you want me to help you and Regina make the improvements so we can sell at the higher price."

"Exactly."

"What happened to the offer you put in on a house?"

"They accepted another one. But the Realtor said, if we make improvements…"

"No, Greg. Enough! You and Regina can make your improvements. You're going to have to buy me out. Either that or sell the damn house as is. Send the papers overnight and I'll sign whatever you want. I just want to be done."

"You're not thinking straight. This is our house!"

"No, it's *your* house. And Regina's. It hasn't been

mine for years. My name is on the deed and that's all. I've allowed this to go on this long but it's over now. Done. I'll take you back to court if I have to."

"That means coming back to Missouri and hiring a family law attorney."

"I'll have to come back anyway to pack and empty my apartment. I can see the lawyer then."

"Be reasonable."

"I'm being incredibly reasonable. Finally."

"I thought we'd settled this. What made you change your mind? Is it that summer dude? You can't go back to your teenage years no matter how much you might have idealized that time in your life. This is the real, grown-up world, and your surfer boy is not going to be able to support you the way I did."

"Support me?" She snorted. "And by support me do you mean control me?"

"Not this again," he groaned.

"For your information, my surfer boy, as you call him, is a former Navy SEAL who could probably kill you with one finger. He owns a business, everyone loves him and he's the best man I've ever known!"

"So you're sleeping with him."

"Argh!"

Valerie hung up because she couldn't listen to another word.

Greg would never stop trying to control her unless she showed him she was done.

Finally, she hoped she'd done exactly that.

Chapter Twenty-Four

A day later, Valerie sent her dad home. He was ready to go, knowing that with every day he spent with Gram he risked all the progress they'd made. Gram kissed him goodbye when he left, calling him a good man, and that his father would be proud of him. Her father nearly wept.

Another meeting of the Almost Dead Poets Society was happening tonight, so Valerie would do a little cleaning and straightening up after dinner. Already all the clutter Gram loved had started to take over her spot by the recliner again. Really, she had to move more often. New goal: get Gram out of that recliner.

Valerie only got out of bed to make Gram breakfast, then she'd retire to her bed where she'd stare at the cracks in her ceiling. Ache some more, try to eat something even if she had no appetite, make Gram lunch, then dinner. Rinse and repeat the next day.

Teachers in Charming were probably already shopping for classroom supplies. Valerie was still waiting to hear from the local district. She'd always looked forward to the end of summer with excitement. At the end of every August she got a brand-new beginning. She thought of August as the new year. Another group of fresh-faced eight-year-olds to mold and teach. Now she had no job, and she had no Cole, either. She saw how her decision not to ask him to come with her might have seemed like she hadn't chosen him. That she hadn't put him first. Nothing could be further from the truth.

But she still didn't know how to make things right, or if she had the courage to risk her heart again. She went back to counting the cracks in the ceiling.

She'd been lying to herself that she could really start her life over again. That by reaching into her past when times were simpler, she'd be able to find joy again. Maybe if Cole hadn't been here, she wouldn't have completely fooled herself into thinking she could find some small part of that young woman, someone who still hadn't made life-altering mistakes. Someone who would have never imagined she'd already have a failed marriage at the ripe old age of thirty-two.

"I'm an old woman who's been through the loss

of my husband, plus a stroke, but you don't see *me* hiding in the bedroom." Gram stood, hands braced on her walker, in the doorway to Valerie's bedroom.

"You are one tough broad," Valerie said, dragging herself out of bed. "Tougher than I am. You do know you have PT today?"

"And I'm going to face it," Gram said, tipping her chin.

"Stop the presses," Valerie said, moving past Gram to the kitchen. She pulled out a mug from the cupboard and shoved it under the coffee machine. Then she pasted a smile on her face. "I'll be awake to cheer you on."

Gram shuffled over in her walker and plopped down at the kitchen table. "Are you going to tell me what happened, or just let me guess?"

"I really don't want to talk about it," Valerie said.

"I've given you three days."

"And?"

"That's all I'm going to give you."

"Gee, that's generous of you."

"Tell me why you don't want to get out of bed."

"Cole and I broke up."

Gram did not look surprised. "I was afraid of that. You have the same look you did every last night of summer vacation, before you were to head back to Missouri the next morning. Like you'd lost your best friend."

"Maybe I did." She plopped down at the table with her coffee. "I loved him when we were kids, and somehow, I got wrapped up in him all over again. But he and I are probably better off as friends."

"Why?"

"Because, I don't know, maybe I love him too much." Valerie couldn't quite put into words the uncomfortable and overwhelming feelings that Cole stirred up in her. "I just… I want something easy and simple. Safe and carefree. Like we used to be together. I thought we could be like we were before, but either I didn't remember how we were, or…"

"Or you're wrong?"

"Wrong. What do you mean, *wrong*?"

"You don't actually want simple or easy. What you want is passion and thrills and deep, lasting love like your Papa and I had. But that also scares you."

She scoffed. "I'm going to save a lot of money on a therapist, I can see."

"I might start charging."

Except for the lack of financial education, Valerie wanted the kind of relationship that her grandparents had. The total love and faith in each other. She loved Cole, and probably always had, of that she had no doubt. But did she trust him?

"How do you do it? How do you have so much faith in someone?"

"Think of it like diving into a swimming pool, honey. You know how to swim, right?"

"Um…yes?"

"Then that's what you do. Just dive in and swim. The moment I met your Papa, I just jumped. He caught me, and I trusted him to catch me every single day after that. Anyway, half the fun is figuring out if you want to do the breaststroke or just doggy paddle."

Okay, so Valerie got the metaphor, though she was having a hard time hanging on to it. "You're comparing a long-lasting romantic relationship to *swimming*?"

Valerie didn't know if she agreed, but she couldn't help but think that Cole would love this analogy.

Later, at the poetry meeting, Gram sat preparing to share with the group her latest poem. The senior citizens began to arrive, Lois and Mr. Finch together, giving more fuel to those rumors that they'd started a relationship. Gram's poem was a not-so-subtle hint to Valerie that love was worth the risk. She ended by describing in detail the first kiss she'd ever had with Valerie's grandfather.

Next, Susannah recited her latest poem about Doodle.

The poem now made Valerie think of Sub. He was a good boy and she wondered what he and his master were doing tonight.

Etta May elbowed Valerie. "Why don't *you* try a poem tonight? Share something with us. Believe me, honey, it's cathartic. Like therapy but free."

"What makes you think I need therapy? Anyway, I couldn't. I'm really not any good."

"The goal isn't to be good. The goal is to express yourself."

"I express creativity with my photos. Not words."

Ever prepared, Etta May pulled out paper and pens from her bag and handed them to Valerie. "You can do it."

Lois's poem was a romantic second-chance love poem, the clean and wholesome version. It further cemented the belief that Lois and Roy had started something, going by the fact that he squirmed uncomfortably. Still, he smiled, something Valerie had seen him do exactly *twice*.

Etta May stood between presenters. "Folks, Valerie will be sharing tonight."

"Um…"

"Wonderful!" Gram said. "We'd love to hear it."

"Hear, hear," said Mr. Finch, clapping.

Valerie continued to scribble on her paper. Unfortunately, all that came to mind was a certain golden-haired bartender with deep blue eyes. His dimpled smile. Long, deep kisses in the steamy shower.

Proving that she was certainly her grandmother's girl.

Mr. Finch recited another moving poem about the Gulf Coast, borrowing heavily from the area's history. To be honest, it sounded a lot more optimistic. Valerie wondered if it was love that had changed him, or maybe some kind of supplement.

After everyone had taken their turn, there was nowhere left to hide.

"Last but not least, let's hear it for Valerie!" Etta May stood.

"C'mon, Valerie!" Mr. Finch clapped. "You've got this."

"Just express yourself," Lois said. "Give us your heart."

"It doesn't have to rhyme!" said Gram. "Look at my poems."

She'd rather not, thank you. If only she had more time, she could come up with something…not horrible. Maybe. But she couldn't share this, which was simply her own version of Gram's erotic poetry. She wished for an interruption of some kind. Maybe a minor hurricane could land right now, just a teeny one, so everyone could be distracted.

"Okay, okay!" Valerie tossed her hands up. "I don't like what I have here, so I'm going to just wing it."

"How daring!" Etta May said. "I absolutely love it."

After all, how many times had she made up speeches in her teaching career? She'd had to speak to groups of parents and families at the start of every year. Open house, and other faculty events. Of course, then she always had material. The syllabus for the year. How parents could help. What they could expect. All things she'd recited so many times she could do it in her sleep.

Now she was supposed to open up her heart and make it pretty, too. Well, she didn't like this.

The teacher in her moved to the front of the room to face everyone. Then she glanced at the warm faces of these people that she'd come to adore in the short time since she'd arrived. She'd arrived only for Gram, never expecting to trust, much less love anyone again.

All these wonderful people here tonight loved and, more important, trusted Cole. And Valerie trusted them. She just didn't know if she had the guts to trust herself and her own instincts anymore. Because if she did, all the possibilities would really open up to her. She might then have everything she'd ever dreamed about.

She took a breath and opened her mouth to speak. Then shut it again. Her lower lip trembled, and she fought to gain control of it. She would not cry here. She would not cry!

It was Lois who cocked her head and noticed that something had gone terribly wrong with Valerie. That the fun and the challenge had gone south like Dixie. Her eyes were solemn, warm and questioning.

And at the kindness in her eyes, Valerie burst into tears.

Lois handed Valerie a wad of tissues.

"What happened to her?" Mr. Finch bellowed.

"She's crying, dummy. Can't you see that?" Lois said, rubbing Valerie's back.

"Someone fix this," Mr. Finch said. "Immediately!"

"I'm so sorry." Etta May wrung her hands together. "I thought this exercise would help, not hurt."

"I sure wish I'd brought Doodle along. No one can cry with Doodle in their lap," Susannah said. "It's physically impossible."

"It's Cole," Gram said, patting Valerie's shoulder. "She loves him, don't you know."

"How sweet," Lois said, batting her eyelashes at Mr. Finch.

"Cole is a good man." Mr. Finch cleared his throat. "You'll find no one better."

They didn't understand and maybe they never could. From another generation entirely, some of the women couldn't see how Valerie had fought her entire adult life to be her own person. To be independent, self-sustaining, reliable. Unbreakable.

"We had something special, so precious. Just like before, I ruined everything."

"As long as you're both still alive, I bet it can be fixed," Gram said.

"I actually *need* him. What if he leaves me someday? What if he gets tired of me?"

"That's a lot of what-ifs," Mr. Finch said. "What if we all get hit by an asteroid tomorrow and Texas is wiped clear off the map?"

"That's interesting, Roy. Will this asteroid also possibly hit the rest of the *world*?" Etta May said, pulling a face.

Valerie stared at both of them, unblinking. "You are not helping."

"Sorry, but it's just as likely that a man like Cole would cheat on his woman as an asteroid would take out Texas. He's been about as different from his father as Texas is from…um, let's see… California."

"I would have said New York," Lois said.

"You've got to stop pushing people who love you away," Gram said. "Being strong doesn't mean you can't be sweet sometimes."

Or that maybe some people were worth the risk. She could, at least for a little while, depend on someone other than herself. Needing him and loving him didn't mean she'd lose herself.

Cole had never been anything more than honest and aboveboard with her and everyone he knew.

"I have to fix this."

Once, in truly dramatic fashion, she'd never wanted to see him again. She could give herself a pass on that due to her youth, but she'd never know what could have happened if she'd kept open to another plan.

This, now, was her Plan B. Her second chance. And she couldn't just let Cole walk away.

All the members of the Almost Dead Poets Society cheered Valerie on as she climbed into Gram's station wagon thirty minutes later. She hadn't bothered changing out of her jeans, tank top and sandals. She'd simply wiped away her tears and smoothed down her hair. Time was suddenly of the essence.

"Go get 'im!" said Gram.

Valerie didn't know that Cole would be at the Salty Dog, but she'd try him there first. She'd tell him the truth: she was *terrified*. But she chose him, and she would every day for the rest of her life. She wanted another chance at forever. She wanted a man she trusted.

This time with the knowledge that she trusted *herself*, too.

Because she couldn't let one abysmal failure determine the rest of her life. Everyone made mistakes and everyone deserved forgiveness. She might make more mistakes in her future, as she tried to let go and trust while hanging on, but Cole would never be one of them.

The boardwalk was crowded, and the parking lot full. She had to park the station wagon at quite a distance. As she walked, she remembered that tonight, all the rides at the wharf were half off, so families were clustered, spilling out onto the boardwalk from the rides. The Ferris wheel, the bumper cars, the merry-go-round. The roller coaster. The sky glider, full of adrenaline freaks, all trying to get to the other side of the boardwalk faster, avoiding the throngs by hanging twenty foot above them. She elbowed teens and children who were dragging their parents to yet another long line.

Finally, she made it to the Salty Dog and saw Debbie. But no Cole.

"Where's Cole?"

"Honey, he left. He's gone."

"What do you mean he's *gone*? Where?"

Max suddenly appeared behind Debbie. "Don't you think you've done enough? Leave him alone. He's going to be fine, no thanks to you."

"Look, I don't have time for this!" She grabbed Max by the shirt collar. "Tell me where he is. Now!"

He slid her a patient look and removed each of her hands with little more than a nudge. "He's gone to a cabin in the country. He won't be back until next week."

"When did he leave?"

"He left a minute ago. You just missed him."

"Ugh! Why didn't you say so?"

She ran, already having wasted precious minutes talking with overprotective Max. It wouldn't be the end of the world if she didn't catch Cole now, because she'd talk to him when he got back. But she didn't want him spending too much time alone, sad, believing that she hadn't chosen him. Maybe even feeling abandoned. She ran, elbowing people along the boardwalk, trying to get ahead of them.

"Hey!" a surly teenager said. "Watch it, lady."

Then she caught sight of Sub ahead, walking dutifully next to his master. Head bent, Cole ambled along with the crowd, hands in his pockets, seemingly in no great hurry.

"Cole!" she screamed just as the roller coaster went by.

If not for all these people here tonight, she'd already have caught up to him. Still, she made progress, ducking under some taller people and continuing to make her way ahead of the pack. Then the bumper car ride let out and a sea of people swarmed ahead.

And she could no longer see Cole or Sub.

Just ahead of her lay the entrance to the sky glider. It looked similar to a ski lift, a dangerous long cable with hanging bucket seats that managed to get people to the other side of the boardwalk. It would probably get her ahead of Cole the way these crowds were moving tonight.

Her legs were only trembling a little as she took a seat on the glider and grabbed on tight to the rail.

Good Lord, the view from up here! *Terrifying*. Another thing she hadn't noticed in the past was that the ride moved slowly. Which was a good thing, she guessed, but not for someone who'd like to get this over with. She sat in the molded plastic seat, nothing but a flimsy barrier keeping her from falling a good twenty or more feet to the ground. Still she hung on to that rail. Her legs dangled with nothing to shield them. No little footrest. Nothing. Just air. She may as well walk out the door stark naked. It might be a little less frightening than this.

She saw Cole straight ahead as the glider moved slowly forward, and lowered her head as much as she dared.

"Cole! Up here! Look!"

He didn't hear her, or if he had he ignored her, and kept walking. Then a child stopped him to pet Sub, and Valerie's chair went right over them.

"Cole!" She let go for a second with one hand just to wave and get his attention and her seat moved an inch, making her scream.

Well, *that* got his attention.

He glanced up and squinted. "Valerie?"

"I choose youuuu!"

"Whaa?" he yelled back.

She thought she might die. Now *everyone* was looking up.

"Hey, isn't that the woman who ran for Mr. Charming?"

"Mom, that lady just screamed." A child pointed. "Should we call 911?"

Her teeth were chattering now from pure adrenaline, and she wrapped her arms around her waist as the chair slowly lowered and she began to return to sweet earth. The glider came to its stop along the platform and she prepared to hop off like everyone else in front of her had.

Cole made his way back to the drop-off point, Sub behind him wagging his tail like it might come off. A few curious people had gathered to watch the crazy lady.

He offered his hand to help her off. "What are you doing?"

"I…I had to catch you before you left."

He narrowed his eyes. "You could have called."

"But I…I wanted to see you." She glanced around at the curious crowd of lookers and cleared her throat. "Um…could we…?"

As if he'd just noticed all the attention she'd called, Cole took Valerie's hand and pulled her off to the side. "What's wrong?"

She grabbed his hands and held them. "I'm sorry. I'm not going anywhere without you. I've been an idiot. But I choose you. I chose you a long time ago, and I will always choose you. Every single day until the day I die. I'm in, I'm all in."

The corner of his mouth quirked up. "You beat me to it. I was going to find you tonight and tell you that *I'm* the idiot."

"You weren't going to the cabin?"

"No, I changed my mind, and I'd returned the keys to Max."

Oh, that Max! He'd lied to her, to make her work for Cole, she imagined.

"This is hard to admit, but I was wrong. I should have never given you an ultimatum. I'm not that guy."

"I know you're not, but you happened to be right about this. I had to *show* you that I'm in." And I do need you, Cole because I love you so much. I never realized that there could be a right way to need someone."

He caressed her hair. "You show me that every day. Because of you, the Salty Dog is still operating. And because of you, I stayed in a silly contest and had one of the best times of my life."

"Me, too."

"I love you, Valerie. I'll show you every day, I swear."

Heart overflowing, Valerie jumped into his arms and he easily caught her.

"But I love you more. I'll show you more. This is one contest I'm determined to win."

Epilogue

Three months later

Cole would say one thing for certain. Life was good when you were in competition with your best friend. Both he and Valerie were trying to outdo each other in the best lover category. When he brought a morning cup of coffee to Valerie, she got up early the next day to cook him pancakes and serve him breakfast in bed. When he bought her a new camera, she bought him a surfboard.

When he bought her a diamond ring, she said yes.

All in all, she just kept besting him, and he'd never been happier.

Best of all, their shower love acrobatics were increasingly…interesting.

She'd moved in last month and he and Sub had adjusted just fine to the only female in their household. Among other things it meant a fully stocked kitchen complete with doggy treats. All in all, he'd never been happier in his life and he'd been a happy guy to begin with. But this was different. A love so deep and pure that complete satisfaction and peace washed over him every day. No matter how difficult life became, he would come home every day to the most beautiful woman in the world. He really didn't deserve her.

"Cole," Ava said from her stool at the bar. "Would you please at least consider it?"

"Sorry. Our wedding is not going to be a Chamber of Commerce event."

"But just think about it! Mr. and Ms. Charming. The mayor would love it. It's perfect!"

"It's private."

There were very few things he would not share with the entire town of Charming and his wedding day was one of them. The honeymoon was another. He glanced over at the plaque that the Chamber of Commerce had awarded him along with the money. In a move that had surprised both him and Valerie, it had been engraved to Mr. and Ms. Charming.

He owed much of this to Ava, who became their champion. She and Valerie were great friends.

Just then the door swung open and in walked his

fiancée, the love of his life, fresh off a day at the private grade school where she currently worked as a substitute teacher. She was high on the list of teachers expected to be offered a contract to teach next May. Ava had used every one of her connections to help Valerie. Until then she still worked part-time at the Salty Dog. She waved to some of their regulars but strutted right up to him and came behind the bar.

Hands fisted in his hair, she kissed him, hard. "We made paper turkeys today."

"I've never heard of anything sexier in my entire life."

He teased her about paper crafts mercilessly because she never seemed happier than when she'd spent a day working with children. They'd already talked about having one of their own because both wanted to start a family immediately.

"Valerie," Ava said. "Can I talk to you about the wedding?"

"Sure, hon." Valerie came out of his arms, but before she went back, he tugged on her wrist and sent her a specific look.

The look said, *Do not make our wedding a Mr. and Ms. Charming event.*

She read him clearly and nodded, because on everything that mattered, they were always in agreement. Solidarity, baby. It meant everything to him. Max hadn't been wrong thinking that Cole expected someone to guard his six. And though he didn't want

Valerie behind him with an Uzi, he did want her to always have his back. Because he had hers. Forever.

It was one of the reasons he'd gone back with her to Missouri. Not just to see her parents and meet her friends, but to help move the last of her stuff. He'd found a digital camera in the back of her closet and made her promise to take more photos. She'd been doing just that, and while there were probably far too many of Sub, he was content that she'd reconnected with one of her passions.

He'd also made it a point to come along to the Realtor with her and Greg. And while Valerie's ex-husband might be a lot of things, stupid wasn't one of them. He'd taken one long look at Cole, the ring on Valerie's finger, and had accepted that the last tie he had to her had been cut. For good.

Cole had tried not to gloat. Too much.

He and Valerie had already been through some tough times with his father, who'd fallen off the wagon less than a month after telling Cole that he'd joined a twelve-step program. Both he and Valerie presented a united front and told Lloyd that he would not be a part of their lives, or their children's lives, until he made it through the program successfully. The day Lloyd had received his 30 Days Sober pin was a big day in the Kinsella lighthouse. Cole had invited him over to celebrate with a cookout and plenty of Coke on hand.

Cole polished a glass as he looked over at the woman who owned his whole heart. She laughed and chatted with Ava, but then glanced over at him and sent him a sweet smile and a sly wink.

It was just one of so many things in his life that he'd never again take for granted.

* * * * *

Try these other great second chance romances,
available now from Harlequin Special Edition:

Starting Over with the Sheriff
By Judy Duarte

Their Second-Chance Baby
By Tara Taylor Quinn

His Secret Starlight Baby
By Michelle Major

And don't miss Heatherly Bell's next book,
Grand-Prize Cowboy
part of the Montana Mavericks:
The Real Cowboys of Bronco Heights continuity.

Coming October 2021!

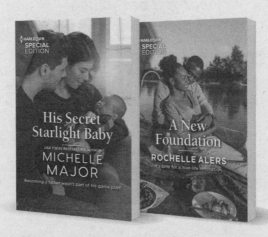

#2845 A BRAMBLEBERRY SUMMER

The Women of Brambleberry House • by RaeAnne Thayne

Rosa Galvez's attraction to Officer Wyatt Townsend is as powerful as the moon's pull on the tides. But with her past, Rosa knows better than to act on her feelings. Yet her solo life is slowly becoming a sun-filled family adventure—until dark secrets threaten to break like a summer storm.

#2846 THE RANCHER'S SUMMER SECRET

Montana Mavericks: The Real Cowboys of Bronco Heights
by Christine Rimmer

Vanessa Cruise is spending her summer working in Bronco. Rekindling her short-term fling with the hottest rancher in town? Not on her to-do list. But the handsome rancher promises to keep their relationship hidden from the town gossips, then finds himself longing for more. Convincing Vanessa he's worth the risk might be the hardest thing he's ever had to do...

#2847 THE MAJOR GETS IT RIGHT

The Camdens of Montana • by Victoria Pade

Working with Clairy McKinnon on her father's memorial tests Major Quinn Camden's every resolve! Clairy is still hurt that General McKinnon mentored Quinn over his own adoring daughter. When their years-long rivalry is replaced by undeniable attraction, Quinn wonders if the general's dying wish is the magic they both need... or if the man's secrets will tear them apart for good.

#2848 NOT THEIR FIRST RODEO

Twin Kings Ranch • by Christy Jeffries

The last thing Sheriff Marcus King needs is his past sneaking back into his present. Years ago, Violet Cortez-Hill disappeared from his life, leaving him with unanswered questions—and a lot of hurt. Now the widowed father of twins finds himself forced to interact with the pretty public defender daily. Is there still a chance to saddle up and ride off into their future?

#2849 THE NIGHT THAT CHANGED EVERYTHING

The Culhanes of Cedar River • by Helen Lacey

Winona Sheehan and Grant Culhane have been BFFs since childhood. So when Winona's sort-of-boyfriend ditches their ill-advised Vegas wedding, Grant is there. Suddenly, Winona trades one groom for another—and Grant's baby is on the way. With a years-long secret crush fulfilled, Winona wonders if her husband is ready for a family...or firmly in the friend zone?

#2850 THE SERGEANT'S MATCHMAKING DOG

Small-Town Sweethearts • by Carrie Nichols

Former Marine Gabe Bishop is focused on readjusting to civilian life. So the last thing he needs is the adorable kid next door bonding with his dog, Radar. The boy's guardian, Addie Miller, is afraid of dogs, so why does she keep coming around? Soon, Gabe finds himself becoming her shoulder to lean on. Could his new neighbors be everything Gabe never knew he needed?

HSECNM0621